W9-BGC-868

ATTACK!

The Penetrator turned his weapon toward Soo Lin. "Is there a loaded magazine for that chatter gun?"

She shouted at him in Chinese and threw the machine gun at him.

Another man had crept toward the back door. Mark blasted a high-speed slug into his side. He flopped once on the floor and lay still. Four of Mark's ten shots were gone. Two more men bolted for the front door, and he cut them down, hitting both in the legs with three shots.

Soo Lin jerked open the door and ran out. He heard her screaming her way down the hall.

Two burp guns chattered in front of him, slugs denting the walls and ceiling. He darted, pulling the white phosphorus grenade from his pocket . . .

The Penetrator Series

#1 THE TARGET IS H

#2 BLOOD ON THE STRIP

#3 CAPITOL HELL

#4 HIJACKING MANHATTAN

THE PENETRATOR
HIJACKING MANHATTAN

by
Lionel Derrick

PINNACLE BOOKS • NEW YORK CITY

THE PENETRATOR: HIJACKING MANHATTAN

Copyright © 1974 by Pinnacle Books, Inc.

All rights reserved, including the right to reproduce this book or portions thereof in any form.

An original Pinnacle Books edition, published for the first time anywhere.

Special acknowledgment to Chet Cunningham

ISBN: 0-523-00338-2

First printing, April 1974

Printed in the United States of America

PINNACLE BOOKS, INC.
275 Madison Avenue
New York, N.Y. 10016

HIJACKING MANHATTAN

PROLOGUE

Mark Hardin is the Penetrator. He did not ask to become a household word across America. He did not seek or relish this notoriety, which splashed his daring over the front pages and television networks of the nation. He was simply doing what he had to do: meeting the criminal structure head-on, trying to smash it piece by piece, man by man, to shatter it at every level he could penetrate.

Nor had he intended to capitalize on his Cheyenne blood to help the mystique grow. He had first used a short arrow as an afterthought, then had begun leaving arrowheads deliberately. They were authentic blue flint chipped arrowheads, which his friend David Red Eagle made back at the Stronghold. He used them as warnings—and sometimes to develop panic in an enemy camp.

Only a few people knew that Mark Hardin was the Penetrator. Whenever possible he avoided contact with the police. This secrecy became more impor-

1

tant as state after state put out wanted notices on him and the F.B.I. charged him with interstate flight. In many cases involving the Mafia and other known criminal elements, Mark acted as judge, jury and executioner to provide swift justice.

▪ Mark Hardin did not magically appear full-blown as a skillful, talented and deadly protector of the weak. He had been mauled, battered, forged and tempered in the rough practicalities of life. Looking back, it seemed to him that he had been seduced into his role. His parents had died in a car crash when he was seven. He barely remembered them. He had lived in a dozen different foster homes in the Los Angeles area by the time he graduated from high school. A football athletic scholarship provided his only means for going on to college. There, in his senior year, gamblers tried to get him to throw a big game. He refused, and the next day he was deliberately mashed and seriously injured in practice. The resulting back problem continued to plague him.

After college he went to work as an insurance investigator but soon found the fast money men after him again. He was offered bribes to conceal facts, to overlook truths. After two years he quit the business and joined the army.

In Vietnam he sharpened his natural ability with small arms and individual weapons. He was talented at devising ways to penetrate the defenses of Viet Cong and North Vietnamese operations. Gradually he developed this infiltration skill into a specialty and became known to military commanders as the best line-crosser in the war. They used him for the toughest jobs; they said he could go through any enemy defense and bring back exactly what they wanted.

After many months of this deadly work, Mark went Stateside to an army intelligence school and eventually returned to Saigon to work in the army's CIC branch, the military counterintelligence operations.

South Vietnam was one big vat of corruption and graft. Much of this involved the siphoning off of military supplies for the flourishing black market. Mark exposed several small operations of this type, then at last found the big one. It was a black-market ring that involved shiploads of military supplies, equipment, arms and ammunition. A two-star general and eleven other U.S. army officers were implicated. Knowing the army brass would protect its own, Mark took his factual evidence of the swindle directly to a friend at the Associated Press News Bureau in Saigon. The top blew off when the story broke in papers across the United States, and Mark was quickly relieved of duty with the CIC.

A week later, five shadowy figures jumped Mark and dragged him into a warehouse where they beat him with boots and pipes, leaving him for dead.

His gut determination to survive and extract vengeance pulled him through. After a long stay in an army hospital, he finally found some peace in a modern mountain hideout in the Calico mountains of Southern California, where no man could track him down. The army rednecks knew he was alive and still wanted to repay him for his "betrayal."

That had been before his work as the Penetrator really began, and it seemed like a thousand years ago. In Washington, D.C., he had challenged the entrenched *Société Internationale d'Élite* and put an end to a plot to assassinate the President of the United States. Casualties had mounted as Mark shot up the secret organization, but soon he was dodging the metropolitan police as well as the club's hired killers. The contest came to a bloody conclusion in Williamsburg, Virginia, with the help of a British army weapon from 1716, a Brown Bess muzzle-loader musket.

Before that there had been a tangle in Las Vegas with the Fraulein, a woman so evil she preyed on innocent young girls who were dedicated to dancing. Her Starmaker Agency turned them into nude dancers in casinos and high-priced prostitutes for the rooms upstairs. The whole operation—and the Pink Pussy Casino—fell in a battle of bullets and blood, but Mark didn't have to pull the final trigger on the Fraulein.

Between each of these furious dramas of death, Mark had returned to the Stronghold in the California mountains, determined to think through some direction for his life, some higher purpose that would be productive and worthwhile. But each time he had seen the sweet face of Donna Morgan and remembered her agony as she burned to death, trapped in the smashed car high in the mountains near Big Bear.

The Los Angeles Mafia family had been behind her death, and they had expected Mark to die in the crash, too. He nearly did, but he had been thrown out of the car as it rolled down the steep embankment. By the time he had regained consciousness, the car was burning fiercely and the Mafia hit men had left.

4

That had been the deciding tragedy in a long list of brushes with the underworld, with crooks and goon squads, and it tilted him into a fight against them all, hoping he could even the score for Donna Morgan, for himself, and for every unfortunate victim of organized criminal activity. He had seen too many friends die in Vietnam to believe he could fight forever; but he was in the battle for as long as he lasted.

Hardin had stormed into Los Angeles and within a month had torn and smashed apart one of the premier Mafia families in the nation, the Scarelli family. Don Pietro Scarelli felt the Penetrator's vengeance as he shot up half the criminal soldiers in town and broke up a multimillion-dollar heroin ring.

Now the battle was about to start again. There were no more doubts. He was fully, firmly, unalterably, committed to fighting every aspect of crime he could find, in any way he could. There would be no final victory for him in this war; he knew that. He might come out ahead in the small skirmishes, as he had done so far, but sooner or later the odds would catch up with him. How many Mafia bullets had missed him already? How many explosions, careening cars and knife thrusts had been just far enough away to spare him? He knew it took only one.

During the game he would take out as many of them as he could. Trite? Of course. After all the killing, life seemed a continuous playing out of a pathetic, imbecilic and distorted scenario. But for as long as he could suck in enough breath, he would take his part in the drama.

David Red Eagle, in the Stronghold near Barstow,

would frown and shake his head at this kind of thinking. He would call Mark a cynic. Red Eagle, a full-blooded Cheyenne Indian, had nursed Mark back to health after the murderous auto crash that killed Donna. It was Red Eagle who had sparked in Mark pride in his heritage, an understanding of his ancestors. The old Cheyenne had educated Mark in the skills the traditional warrior of his people must possess.

He also learned some of the rituals and the protections of *Sho-tu-ca*. These mind and body disciplines of the ancient Cheyennes had captivated him. He found they could heighten his senses of sight and hearing. Perhaps they could help him during his battles as they had helped the Cheyenne Indian Dog Soldiers a hundred years ago.

Mark knew that even Professor Haskins would lift one thin white brow at Mark's constant mental examination of his position. The professor was a practical man, a retired university science professor. He had taken Mark in on a friend's recommendation, and soon Mark had been invited to stay and join the Stronghold.

Years before, the professor had built his retreat deep in the barren, almost inaccessible desert mountains. Now the three men formed a troika, a three-way pact, and created a smoothly working team to do battle with crime wherever it was found.

The professor served as intelligence man, researcher, and supplier of outside contacts as well as developer of special weapons such as Ava, the small tranquilizer gun. David Red Eagle tutored Mark in the skills of the unarmed Indian fighter, schooled him in *Sho-tu-ca* and watched his diet. Mark was the outside man, the action, the assault force.

Very often Mark thought back to those three months of joy and tenderness he had experienced when he was with Donna Morgan. She was the professor's niece, and worked as a research assistant in the anthropology department at the University of Southern California. He could still see her gentle smile, which often turned into a soft laugh. He remembered the pixielike arching of her brows, her abrupt way of breaking into a run, and the sudden, silly, funny things she did to see him first smile, and then laugh. At last he closed his eyes tightly and his hands doubled into fists as he began thinking about a new assignment, another mission. There *had* to be some other way to strike back at the criminal structure, and at this atmosphere of permissiveness that spawned so much crime—and the Mafia with it.

Now Mark turned, slid out of his khaki shorts and stepped into the Indian sweatlodge which David Red Eagle had constructed far down one of the old mine tunnels, where it met a flooded shaft. Smoke streamed out the lodge top and up an air shaft toward the top of the mountain.

Inside the lodge a ruddy glow was cast by the round bed of red-hot coals at the center of the cedar-and-deerskin structure. Suspended over the coals stood a platform of iron strips, covered with a layer of small round stones. Mark moved close to the fire, then threw water on the hot stones and sucked in the instant steam.

He thought of all he had concentrated on during the past two weeks of work and study. He had memorized critical and evaluative briefings by the professor on national and world affairs. He had speed-read selected material the professor had marked for him, and he had continued his physical training until he could run two miles through the desert heat in twelve minutes. For hours he had stalked Red Eagle, and only after many tries had he approached through a stone- and leaf-strewn gully undetected. The old Indian's frown had changed to a quiet smile.

Now as a gush of steam billowed up from the rocks, he knew he was ready for a new assignment. He sat, cross-legged, and threw more water on the stones. The professor had said something about New York, and had looked worried at lunch.

Mark tried to forget it and relax. Soon enough he would be moving, anxious, eager to get back into action. He would give the enemy no warning; his strike would be hard, fast, deadly. Many of those on the wrong side of the law would be nervous, unsettled, watching over their shoulders, because they knew the Penetrator was in action again.

1

CLEAR THE TRACKS

The time was 3:30 A.M. on a chilly January night in New York City. Gusty slashes of raw wind hustled a tabloid newspaper page along the deserted street. Two identical small van trucks stopped in no-parking zones near the entrances to the I.R.T. subway at 72nd Street, one on each side of Broadway. The drivers turned off the truck motors and listened for noises that would signal a train entering the station below. The ground shook briefly as heavy sounds came through the air grates at street level. The men checked their watches; one minute after the train rumbled away, they jumped from their trucks. Quickly they removed wooden barricades from the vans and blocked both entrances to the station.

"CLOSED FOR CONSTRUCTION" the placards read. The men walked briskly down the steps to the small boarding platforms flanking the tracks. The time was exactly 3:31.10 as they moved across the dingy ceramic tile on the train level, walking toward the kiosks where tokens were sold.

The smallest of the four men was black, and stood barely five feet tall. He scowled at the dirty station, the trash, the accumulation of years of soot and smoke and the residue of millions of hands and feet.

He checked the platform. Their luck held: no late New Yorkers were waiting for a train downtown or uptown. In unison the four pulled kerchiefs over their faces, leaped in front of the token sellers on each side of the tracks and sprayed mace into the cages until the two workers crumpled to the floor. It was 3:31.15.

The station was still deserted. The attackers glanced at each other, then continued with their well-prepared and rehearsed plan. Simultaneously they forced open the trainmen's room doors and found both spaces empty. At once they turned and sprinted to the turnstiles, vaulted them and ran to the tracks.

The train which had just left had been ninety-six seconds late on its scheduled stop. Another car was not due in from either direction for eight and a half minutes. But they knew the New York subway couldn't be relied on to stay even close to its time-tables this late at night when most cars ran empty.

One man on each platform carried a light green cloth bag. These two jumped between the tracks, being careful not to touch the electrified third rail. Rapidly they bent, set dials, then placed the heavy packages under the train rails, near switches. Their work done, they leaped out of the sunken rail area.

The men signaled each other, then joined the second pair of men who had been working around the main roof supports. These were large concrete and steel columns that held up the street overhead. Rapidly, efficiently and silently they strapped heavy charges to the columns until five on each side of the tracks were prepared. One man on each platform ran from column to column, setting timers, allowing for the five-second differential, as they had done dozens of times in practice. They moved like mirror images of each other on each side of the gleaming steel rails.

By the time the last of the electrical fuses had been set, the other men had broken in the doors of the booths and dragged out the blinded, weeping and blubbering workmen. Both ticket sellers were carried up the stairs.

The drugged I.R.T. workers were dumped on the sidewalk outside the barricades, and the four men walked for their trucks. They took little notice of a pair of heroin shooters in "Needle Park," as the small bit of greenery near the subway was called, but stepped into the waiting vans and drove away. It was exactly 3:36.58, less than six minutes since they entered the underground area, and well within their safety range.

The vans were a half-block down Broadway, driving in opposite directions away from 72nd Street, when the first blast went off under the street in the I.R.T. station.

The explosion fractured the tracks, stripping them from their spikes and binders and curling the heavy steel rails toward the ceiling. They hung there for only a fraction of a second before the first charges along the major support pillars exploded. The heavy concentration of high explosives sheared away the

11

cement and steel columns as if they were melting ice cream bars. In one great whoosh of smoke, dust and hissing steam, a large section of Broadway dropped into the station. That part of the long cave turned into a horrendous tangle of steel, broken pipes, jetting steam, tangled communications cables and sparking electric wires mixed with masses of New York city soil, rocks, and slabs of macadam and cement paving from the street overhead.

A step-van milk truck headed for its early morning rounds skidded all four wheels trying to avoid the cave-in; but its momentum carried it two feet too far. The blunt-nosed rig tilted forward and rolled eight feet down the slanting street into a subway light fixture.

Forty-eight seconds later both vans drove north on Broadway, keeping two blocks apart. Turning at 120th Street, they jogged past Columbia University to Amsterdam Avenue, continued north to 125th Street, and then vanished into the bowels of Harlem. On East 132nd Street, within an oarlock throw of the Harlem River, the drivers eased the vans through an open warehouse door. It was black inside when the lights of the trucks were turned off and the big door dropped down behind them.

Ten seconds later lights snapped on inside the building, and the men crawled from the trucks. No one said a word. Efficiently the four washed down both rigs, wiped them dry, then jacked them up and changed all eight tires and wheels. Twenty minutes later each truck had been professionally painted a metallic blue and driven into a two-truck paint-drying oven where infrared heat lamps glowed brightly.

Only then did the four men begin to relax.

"Smoke 'em," the smallest of the quartet said. His name was Abdul Daley, and there was no doubt he was the leader. He frowned as he peered at the men through his wire-frame glasses. His eyes were cold black nuggets. Daley nodded, then unbuttoned his shirt and stripped it off his slight black body. Without further orders the other men began undressing. Two of them were also black, and their dark skin glistened from the work. The fourth man, a Chinese with shoulder-length hair, took off his shirt and looked at Daley.

"Every damn thing?"

The small man stared at him in surprise; the start of anger showed, but he beat it down. "Yeah, every stitch, especially your shoes. No honkey cop microscope is gonna connect us in any way with that 72nd Street station."

When all four were naked, they took the box of shoes and clothes to the far side of the building and down a stairway to a large, gas-fired incinerator. It turned the garments to ashes in seconds.

Satisfied, Daley led the men to another section of the building and through a door to a table holding four bundles. Each man's name was on one package. They contained new clothes, all carefully sized and styled to fit each individual's temperament and flair.

"Hey, man, you got us some heavy threads, know that?" one man said, a smile covering his broad flat face.

"Right on, brother. Look at these damn flares."

Daley did not smile. He seldom smiled. Now he only dipped his head curtly, and rubbed back a greased-down strand of hair that had escaped from his neatly combed duck's ass haircut. When the others were dressed he led them to another room and pointed to a table filled with hot food and a dozen different kinds of drinks.

"Eat up, brothers. One damn fine job."

Abdul watched them run to the table and grab the bottles, then he turned and went through a door, down a long hall and into another room furnished like a small flat. A naked Chinese girl lay on the round bed. She stirred on the blue satin sheets as the lights came on, then she sat up.

"Abdul, baby! How'd it go?" She stretched like a waking kitten.

"Beautiful, Soo Lin, beautiful."

She jumped off the bed and ran to him, hugging him tightly, remembering to bend her knees so she wouldn't be taller than he.

"Yeah, one crazy, wild bang!" He caught one of her swaying breasts. "Yeah, no foulups, no problems. One beautiful big smash job. No motha-fuckers gonna be using the damned I.R.T. through there for six months!"

"Ab, honey, I knew you could do it!" She kissed him.

He pushed her away and picked up a small radio, which he snapped on. An announcer's voice came across fast, strong and heavy, as if it had a soul sound all its own.

"Oh, yeah, you mamas out there. Give old Squirley a call right now, got some lines open. Tell Big Black Daddy Squirley what's achin' your pretty little black female bones. Get on that horn right now sweetheart, and feed Big Black Squirley the straight goods. I mean rap right on about anything from

14

your sex life and why you ain't getting any. Rap, sweet mama, rap's the name of this heavy game. We chew it till five every early morning. The ever-loving number is 132-4080, so get on it. Got a five minute rap limit, mamas. Now get your undies washed and hung up and give me a rattle on the old honker, ya'll hear?"

"Oh, turn him off," the girl said making a face.

"No way, mama. I'm gonna call Big Daddy and lay a blockbuster on him. The word is going out right now!"

"Hey, wild. No lie?" She brightened and pushed closer against his naked body. "Can I . . . I mean, well, can I listen?"

The small black man nodded, tossed his bundle of clothes on a chair and reached for the phone. After he dialed the number he'd just heard, a voice came over the line, booming above the soul record in the background.

"Turn down your radio, stupid!" Big Daddy Squirley said.

"Shut up, you black bootlicker, and listen. You want a news story? This one could make you famous. Listen to this. Get your recording button ready so you can tape. You'll be able to sell the damn tape all over town tomorrow. Don't interrupt, just listen.

"The Seventy-Second Street I.R.T. station got itself blown to hell tonight, at exactly 3:37 A.M. No traffic gonna go up or down there for six months. Not a single honkey got killed. Wanted to show you what we can do. I mean, it's like a warning, man. You dig? We're striking for racial freedom, and equality. Yeah. We're the *Eusi Dhahabu*. We showin'

15

the city fathers how easy it is to blow up this whole damn island. Tomorrow at noon, man, right on this squawk box, I'm gonna read the list what them honkeys gotta do. Dig? They don't do like we say, we gonna blow up twelve subway stations. We'll knock out every motha-swinging subway into Manhattan. Remember us, Eusi Dhahabu, equal justice for all men."

Abdul put down the phone quickly, even though he knew the radio station would not have had the time or connections to get the call traced. But somehow he felt jeopardized as long as he was plugged into the outside world. He felt more secure here within this small fortress.

Abdul turned up the volume on Big Daddy Squirley's program and heard only loud soul music. A minute later the record ended.

"Hey, mamas, I hit it big. I just taped a wild cat. I'll get it on the air soon as I clean it up a little. But for openers, don't plan on using the Broadway I.R.T. line past 72nd Street tomorrow. I hear they just had an explosion there."

Abdul Daley turned off the radio and stared at it. He shivered. It had begun. After a year of planning and preparing, they were on the attack. He trembled and reached for the softness of the woman. He had earned a little relaxation. She laughed excitedly and pulled him down to the satin sheet on the big round bed.

Lt. Larry Butler sat at his desk in the 59th Street precinct house. It was 3:31 a.m. He tried to concentrate on the material in front of him. He hated this shift. Too much happened for a while, then almost nothing. He sipped the coffee which usually kept him awake. As a lieutenant in the plainclothes division he was supposed to know everything that went on in his sector. He shrugged. He couldn't know half of one percent of what was jiving out there.

He picked up a special police network bulletin and scanned it. This guy was unreal. Larry read the cryptic report. It had come in on the teletype last night and this was the first time he'd had a chance to dig into it. The thin yellow paper and the capital letters irritated him. But this was from the Criminal Intelligence and Identification boys and it caught his eye.

FROM: CII DCMPD: NOTICE TO NORTH AMERICAN CRIME REVIEW NETWORK. HIGHEST PRIORITY. RE: THE PENETRATOR. SUBJECT UNKNOWN BY REAL NAME OR OTHER ALIAS. MAY HAVE BEEN ARMY WEAPONS AND COMBAT EXPERT IN VIETNAM. FIRST APPEARANCE IN LOS ANGELES. BROKE UP MAJOR HEROIN PIPELINE.

SAID TO BE KILLER BUT NO CONCRETE EVIDENCE TIES HIM TO ANY HOMICIDE. SPECIALIZES IN ATTACKING CRIMINALS, ANYONE FLAGRANTLY OUTSIDE THE LAW. DOES NOT FIRE AT PEACE OFFICERS. DEADLY WITH PISTOL, RIFLE, KNIFE, GRENADE LAUNCHER AS WELL AS ALL EXPLOSIVES.

LAST OPERATION, WASHINGTON D.C. BELIEVED STILL OPERATING EAST COAST. USUALLY WORKS ALONE, BUT THOUGHT TO HAVE BACK-UP TEAM.

TRADEMARK: AN AUTHENTIC INDIAN ARROWHEAD OF BLUE FLINT, ABOUT TWO

17

INCHES LONG. OFTEN LEFT AS CALLING CARD AND TO INTIMIDATE TARGETS.

NO OUTSTANDING WARRANTS. IDENTITY UNDETERMINED. FINGERPRINTS DO NOT MATCH ORIGINAL SUSPECT WHO HAS BEEN CLEARED. ARMED AND CONSIDERED HIGHLY DANGEROUS.

IF APPREHENDED HOLD FOR WASHINGTON METROPOLITAN POLICE, ALSO LAS VEGAS, AND LOS ANGELES. ANY CONTACT WITH, OR ACTION BY THE SUBJECT SHOULD BE REPORTED TO LT. KELLY PATTERSON, LA SHERIFF, AND DAN GRIGGS, US JUSTICE DEPARTMENT, WDC.

Lt. Butler pitched the yellow sheet at his "in" basket and sighed. Just what he needed, a deadly, body-dropping nut running around in his private looney bin here in the Fifty-Ninth. That guy had to be a nut. No sweat, he'd never last long enough to work his way to New York. Lt. Butler checked his watch. It was thirty-nine minutes after three. His phone rang.

"Yeah, Butler. Sure. What? Street caved in over a subway station? Right. And get some units down there now. Ambulances and at least ten squad cars. Block off traffic. I'm on my way."

Lt. Butler brushed the .38 snuggled in his shoulder holster and went down the steps three at a time. He knew he was going to break an ankle doing that sometime, but until he did he'd keep running down the damn stairs. He didn't know what had happened up at Seventy-Second and Broadway, but it was a problem he could deal with. He slid into his unmarked cruiser and charged up the street.

He thought about the Penetrator as he drove. The guy was crazy, a one-man war against crime. If he showed up in this precinct he'd get his ears pinned to a door fast.

A cave-in, damn, that could be bad. And no subway traffic tomorrow morning would cause a hell of a traffic jam. But what the hell did the desk man mean about explosions being heard?

Lt. Butler wiped one hand over his rough face as he raced up Broadway, the juices beginning to seep into his gut. This was his kind of emergency, not some will-o'-the-wisp crime fighter who called himself the Penetrator. It was a thousand to one he'd ever see that guy. Lt. Butler hit the siren. Now the acid was really churning in his stomach.

2

BACKLASH VIGILANTES

Mark Hardin flew the Twin Beechcraft Baron into New York's La Guardia Airport a little before noon on Monday. He was there on a fact-finding mission, but came with full battle equipment just in case. That was partly why they had decided to buy a good private plane, so Mark could transport his arsenal and suitcases full of surprise packages without having to submit to the probing of airport security guards. They had wanted a small Lear jet, but that required a co-pilot according to FAA regulations, so they chose the Beech.

Mark knew this trip could be a false alarm. He was investigating "Black Gold," a splinter Negro group some thought had broken off from the Black Panthers. Mark had first heard the name from the taped confession of Lt. Col. Clevon Harris, U.S.A.F., during his hit in Washington, D.C. Harris had been a high-ranking member of S.I.E. and a black. Now

20

Harris was dead, but Black Gold could be very much alive.

The professor had heard the name from a colleague on the staff of New York's Columbia University. The teacher, Dr. Durward Toombs, had been frantic in his concern and alarm about the unrest at the college. He said he'd lived through the student dissent and riots in the sixties, but he hadn't seen anything with this violence quotient.

Professor Haskins had shown Mark part of the letter:

"This sudden rash of building seizures, window breaking, student deaths, and agitation for non-academic black and Chinese studies programs is not only unrealistic, but merges on the frantic, fantastic and fanatic. The basic attitude of the vast majority of students here has changed. It has settled and stabilized, with young people serious about academic pursuits, eager to get their degrees. I have no fear of mass student anarchy. On the contrary, I'm afraid for the protesters. We don't know who killed the two students, but it was done viciously, sadistically. There is a strong backlash here against this small student group, which may number only about thirty. Violence could easily erupt from a backlash vigilante sentiment growing rapidly on campus against this Afro-Chinese alliance."

That had led to a phone call by the professor, and then a second call to a black newspaper editor in Harlem. Professor Haskins had come to Mark three nights ago.

"Mark, I'm not totally satisfied by my talks with these men in New York, and it all points to a highly serious problem that seems to be building."

21

"The Black Gold thing?"

"Precisely. I talked to a friend in Harlem, John Washington. I've learned to trust John. And what he told me is most distressing. He says an extremist group of black militants has sprung up in Harlem that none of the cooler heads can control. There seems to be a strong tie-in with some Chinese radical group, and no one, not even the black power structure, can infiltrate it. So far the police have blamed five homicides on the alliance. They don't have a name for them, and no legal proof of the killings."

"Is it the Black Gold outfit?"

"Nobody seems to know."

"You think I should go check it out?"

"Yes, Mark. I've talked to Red Eagle about it and he agrees. Washington says he's afraid if the top does blow off this thing, it will start so fast and be so ugly the police won't be able to move quickly enough to stop it."

"He have any names, any specifics?"

"No, and that's what worries me. They were only feelings, testings of the air, generalities, extrapolations. But I've known John for years, and he's a man who can literally smell trouble."

Mark remembered it all as he drove toward the heart of the sprawling city. He swung the rented car into the Queens-Midtown Tunnel, gulping down a last lungful of comparatively fresh air before he plunged into the artificial underground soup.

Here he was on another intelligence-gathering mission, like hundreds he had made in 'Nam. Only this time he was on his own home ground, and it

22

was a cold war, so far; but one which could explode into a hot one.

He gave his semi-permeable plastic gloves a tug, smoothing down the thin material at the wrist. He was never without them outside the Stronghold. They provided him with a changing set of fingerprints. He shaved his hands to the wrists twice a week because the gloves themselves had freckles, raised veins and hairs that matched his own skin. You could shake hands with Mark and never know he wore them, they were that good. The fingerprints, especially manufactured into the plastic, were composites of carefully made artists' drawings, and not on file anywhere. Each mission called for a new pair of gloves. He burned the used pair as soon as he returned to the Stronghold. It was one more mechanical technique to help him stay anonymous— and out of jail.

Mark Hardin was a larger, more powerful man than he seemed to be at first glance. At six feet two he was heavily muscled and looked like an athlete in training. His general complexion was dark and he suntanned to a coppery brown when he had a chance. He could move with the supple litheness of a cougar, and his dark eyes and thick black moustache gave his face, even in repose, a smoldering, angry look. When he frowned a sudden lethal aura seemed to surround him.

His hair was black and a little shaggy, hiding part of his ears and fighting with his collar. His best weight was 185 pounds, which he maintained without conscious effort. His accent, if any, was NBC-news-commentator, but Easterners and those from the South picked up a far-West twang if they lis-

23

tened closely. Mark's enemies seldom caught that nuance, since they usually never had a chance to listen at all.

Mark drove out of the tunnel and turned toward 44th Street. After a few indecisive moments, he angled the Lincoln Continental Mark IV in the right direction. He touched the clip holster on his right hip. He'd put the Hi-Standard .22 automatic in the leather holster at the airport. He didn't think he'd need it yet, but somehow he felt better with it under his jacket.

Mark parked in front of the Algonquin Hotel, locked the glove compartment, and slid the trunk key off the ring, putting it in his pocket. He grabbed his suitcase and waved at the doorman.

"Yes sir?"

"Have it parked," Mark said, dropping the ignition key in the man's hand. He headed for the entrance. The doorman took his luggage, called a parking attendant and hurried to open the door for him.

Ten minutes later, Mark relaxed in the big room of the famous old writers' and actors' hotel. He snapped on the television set and caught the noon news.

The camera panned across a war zone; a gaping hole showed in the middle of a street, and work crews scurried around removing debris. The announcer faded in.

"And so that's all that's left of the 72nd Street subway station in Manhattan today after an extremist group blew it up early this morning. No one was injured. The same small Black-Chinese alliance threatened the city of New York with twelve more such bombings, which could totally paralyze subway travel in and out of Manhattan. They are demanding two million dollars in unmarked, used, twenty-dollar bills. The name of the group claiming credit is *Eusi Dhahabu*. Our research people say the name is Swahili and means Black Gold."

The newscaster went on to tell of reactions by the mayor and city councilmen. Mark turned it off. His mouth tightened. So Black Gold was more than just some wild imaginative raving. They had hit already and threatened more, a big ripoff, an actual hijacking of a whole city government.

Mark made the decision automatically. The mission was no longer information and intelligence; it was a full-scale action project.

First he should check on that blown-up station. It might tell him something. He put on a pair of old slacks, a sport shirt and a light jacket, then went to the lobby and asked a bellboy to take him to the hotel engineer. A ten-dollar bill provided an instant response. Five minutes later, carrying an aluminum hard hat on loan from the engineer, Mark ransomed his Continental from the parking attendant.

His only weapon was the .22 Hi-Standard on his hip. Among the papers the professor had worked up for him was a Los Angeles concealed-weapons permit. It would hold up under a quick inspection, but not a complete one.

The rest of his weapons were safe in the trunk of the car. He had kept the trunk key and locked the glove compartment, so the remote release in the glove box could not be activated. That denied the parking boys even a snoop in the trunk without breaking it open.

Mark cruised past the scene at 72nd and Broad-

25

way. Confusion dominated the whole scene. Dump trucks jockeyed in toward the edge of the hole. Electric shovels worked their way into the middle of the depression, chewing out voids in the mass of twisted metal, broken concrete, rocks, dirt and wiring. He checked the area carefully but could see no official-looking delegation. Maybe later. He passed on by. Half an hour later he found the address he wanted on 127th Street.

The area had degenerated into a tentative slum, a ghetto for blacks and Spanish. Half the storefronts had been boarded up or papered over. One or two businesses struggled to maintain their rent payments. A paper sack of take-out Chinese food leftovers thrown on the sidewalk the previous night had been kicked and scattered for half a block. A two-quart cardboard milk carton lay squashed next to the building. Two wine bottles had shattered across the sidewalk nearby. A dozen men sat on the curb near the far end of the block.

Two doors down, a faith healer's neon sign blinked on and off in the full glare of daylight.

Mark checked the number on the door of the nearest building and saw it was the one he wanted. He got out, locked the Lincoln pointedly and turned to eye the two teenage black boys leaning against the wall.

Mark motioned to them. One shrugged and walked over. The other one made a one-fingered gesture and wandered the other way.

"Hey, man, you want me?"

"Yeah. Wanna earn yourself a couple of dollars? Just see that my wheels ain't ripped off or my paint job scratched. Got some business inside with brother Washington."

"Yeah? Whatfo'?"

"Business, man." He checked the street again, then walked toward the door. On the window, patched with torn paper, he saw the lettering: "The Voice of Harlem. Your only truly INDEPENDENT newspaper."

As soon as Mark opened the door he was flooded with the unmistakable scent he associated with all newspapers—that sharp, dusty, semi-basement smell of raw newsprint. It filled every nook and crevice in the small front office when he went inside. The room had new lights, serviceable furniture, a counter holding stacks of last week's issue, and a half-dozen office cubicles on one side. A black girl behind a typewriter at the counter looked up as he came in.

"Help you?" she asked.

"Yes—Mr. Washington?"

"Back there," she said, waving toward the last small rectangle of an office. Mark found a man bent over a sheaf of galley proofs with a heavy copy pencil in his hand.

"Mr. Washington?"

He was a small man, black as the inside of one of his ink cans, with large metal-framed glasses perched on his nose. His head produced a rich crop of tight, kinky black hair, and his ears looked like large eggplant slices.

The editor's shirt sleeves had been rolled up two turns, and wide red suspenders held up his pants. He lowered the pencil and looked up, staring at this new interruption.

27

"You got to be a cop or a football player. Tight end, maybe, or a flanker back. You're big, that's for damn sure. With that tan you must be from Las Vegas or Californa. Which could make your name Henry Joerden."

Mark grinned and sat in the chair Washington pointed to beside his battered desk. "Mr. Washington, what I hear about you must all be true."

The small man stared at Mark without acknowledging the compliment.

"You're here about Black Gold. It's one damn big mess right now. They started it, and all hell is breaking loose, but it's just the beginning, that's my guess. You saw the blast job they did at 72nd Street?"

"Yes," Mark said. He liked this fiery little black man; now what he needed were some hard facts.

"Mr. Washington, you know I'm doing some research for Professor Haskins . . ."

A chuckle from Washington stopped Mark. "Son, you look about as much like a leg man as I do a fullback for the Jets." He took a deep breath, shrugged, then looked at Mark again. "What the hell, if you can help with this mess, straighten out any of it . . ."

"What I need are some names, a meeting place, some backers, anything to get that first little handle."

Washington got up and paced the narrow hallway, then came back. Typewriters continued to clatter around them. The editor dropped into his chair, his face sad.

"All I can tell you is what I told the special anti-riot unit from the police this morning. I don't have any names except one. These people are black ghosts that move in the night, making contacts, leaving literature. Sometimes they push a full-blown news story under my door, all written up in the right form, and with some thought and talent behind it. We print them with a note about how we got them. But names ..."

He took a pipe from an ash tray and began digging into the bowl to clean it. "The only name of any kind I got is Soo Lin. She went to Columbia for a while and was in the middle of the Chinese People's movement on campus. But she vanished two months ago. Nobody's seen her since."

"What about the bars they hang out in—a dive, a beer joint? You must have something on them."

"Not a whisper. It's never been like this before. People usually talk a lot, we've always heard *before* something is going to break. But not this time. It's like it was a secret club. And you won't get to first base in this end of town, not with that damn honkey face of yours hanging out." He grinned as he said it and Mark laughed.

"So I've got no place to start. Can they work it? Can they get that two-million dollar ripoff?"

"They just might," Washington said. He stood again, worry lines wrinkling his forehead. "That job last night was smooth, like a commando raid. Nobody saw anybody go in or come out. The ticket sellers were gassed and hauled outside, so nobody got killed. They hit just after one train left and before the next one was due. It had all the touch of military precision. A hell of a lot of planning went into that one. I think they'll convince the mayor, and the police commissioner. Hell, it'll cost more than two million to rebuild that one subway station."

Mark scowled. "That's what I was afraid you were

going to say. What about the homicides? The professor said they think the outfit has killed five times."

Washington sat down and leaned back in the swivel chair. "Probably only twice. Some inner-organizational row as near as we can figure. Not a trace of evidence. Both men were stripped and dumped in the river. It was a miracle either one was identified. The hands were cut off both men and never found. Finally they got an I.D. through partial facial structure, and then dental X-ray records."

"Sounds like a quaint little social club."

"Whoever they are, they aren't kidding. If this outfit says it will do something, we better believe it will. I wish I could give you something more."

Mark stood, shook hands with Washington and thanked him.

"Oh, Joerden," Washington said. "If you do happen to turn up anything, I'd love to scoop the *New York Times* on something, just once. Give me a call."

"Maybe I could slip something under your front door," Mark said, and waved as he walked away.

Outside, Mark found his Continental Mark IV the center of attraction for ten young boys. One, about six, rushed up to him.

"Hey, man. That big dude working for you? You paying his ass?"

Mark nodded.

"Then, man, you got to pay me too, cause I helped him."

Mark leaned down, caught the boy and lifted him by the ankles into the air, his head hanging down. Mark shook him until change began falling from his pockets. The other boys scrambled around on the sidewalk for the pennies and nickles.

Mark put him down gently on the sidewalk and saw tears close to spilling from dark brown eyes. After giving the older boy two dollars, Mark slipped one folded dollar bill into the six-year-old's hand, then slid into the big car.

He drove sixty blocks south, then parked as close as he could to the blasted subway station, and taking his hard hat, walked down where he could get a good look. The near end seemed to be the center of activity, and as he watched, two big black limousines pulled up and stopped. Four men in suits and carrying hard hats got out. Mark decided it had to be some kind of official inspection party.

He put on his hard hat and began walking quickly after the men. If he stuck close enough to them he should be able to slip in without any questions asked. Most of the construction workers had left. There had to be some lead here, a small fact that might give him a place to start unraveling this mystery.

3

C-4 = NO MORE!

Mark kept a hundred feet in back of the official party as it moved into the area. They passed a policeman manning a guard post near the edge of the wreckage. Mark slowed his steps, waiting until the quartet came to the edge of the subway steps marked "Downtown."

"Hey, you can't come in here," the cop barked.

Mark kept moving toward him, but slowed and grinned.

"Sorry, I can't keep up with the boss. He told me to get my tin pot on and that put me behind the others . . ."

The cop scowled. "What the hell you talking about? This is a restricted zone."

"It's alright, officer. I'm with that group ahead. Some stupid inspection trip, and I got dragged along. I'm Con Edison, planning department, and I got a call from my boss to be down here to go along and take notes."

"They didn't tell me anything about anybody else, just Councilman Andreeson and his party." The cop paused, then looked at the heads of the councilman's foursome going down the stairs. "You got any identification?"

Mark's manner suddenly changed. "Look, man, don't hassle me. I didn't want to come anyway. I'll just take your damn badge number and tell my people you wouldn't let me in."

"All I need is some identification."

"Sure, Con Edison pins little badges on us with numbers and our pictures, just like a cop carries, or an army dude. But that's just for guys in the field, not us front office types. You think you're still in the service? Now let me in or keep me out, I don't give a damn which. Just make up your mind."

The cop was five-ten. He stared up at Mark's six-two frame, at the sudden anger in his face. The blue-coat shrugged.

"What the hell, I'm not going to get my ass in a sling over a dumb damn thing like this. Go ahead."

Mark was grumbling about cops overstepping their authority as he walked quickly past him and toward the remains of the 72nd Street subway station. The stairway led to the only part of the platform not totally wrecked. The strong cement work and tons of earth on top had protected it, shooting the main force of the blast toward the other side, and down the length of the tunnel. He picked his way down the steps, covered with fallen concrete, dust, rocks and dirt. It was after three o'clock and the construction workers were done for the day. Mark made it to the bottom of the stairs and stared at the massive destruction. It reminded him of some of the larger buildings he'd seen at Hue after the Tet offensive.

The councilman's group stood another fifty feet ahead, around all that was left of one of the massive concrete and steel pillars that had held up the street. The shattered stub had been exposed as they dug out the rubble.

Mark moved toward them, checking what was left of the ceiling structure, and the masses of twisted cables, pipes, wires and beams. As he came within fifteen feet of them, someone called.

"Hey, you! What the hell you doing down here?"

Mark stared at a maze of wires for a moment, made a note on a small pad from his pocket, then turned.

"Me? You talking to me?"

"Yeah, you."

"Con Edison. I've got to get a prelim eval out on this by six o'clock. I told Mr. Hart that wasn't time enough, but he said get down here and do it. You know the trouble we're having with restoring service. He said this would help. Oh, my name is Joerden."

The man who had called now frowned. Dammit, he didn't remember anything about an evaluation report from the utility. Or was it *for* Con Edison? They were up to their generators just trying to restore temporary service to half a block of small businesses fed by this outdated, underground wiring. And the sooner they got the regular traffic lights working, the sooner he could pull some patrolmen off traffic duty.

Lt. Larry Butler, NYPD, stared at the big, deeply tanned man. Must just be back from Florida. He nodded his permission for him to stay, then turned back to the group. Councilman Andreeson was saying something. The big stiff hardly ever said anything worth listening to.

"Gentlemen, we've had our lab men work over this pillar with everything we've got. They say some type of heavy satchel charges were strapped around the pillars. There is no doubt in their minds that it was plastic C-4 explosive that tore this station apart. Probably nearly two hundred pounds of it."

Police Commissioner Randy McNeely snorted. "You guys are off your marbles. That's restricted stuff. Nobody gets C-4 but the army and maybe some National Guard outfits."

McNeely was six feet tall, and heavy. He weighed over two hundred and eighty pounds and bragged about how much he could eat of anything, from spaghetti and pizza to apple pie and ice cream. He claimed the Bronx record for downing a 24-ounce pitcher of beer in 7.5 seconds.

"Face it, Andreeson," the Commissioner said. "Your boys goofed, it couldn't have been C-4."

Councilman Andreeson snorted softly and looked at the fat man. He never had liked McNeely. "Just because something is illegal, Commissioner, doesn't mean it isn't happening. And just because C-4 is illegal to sell, doesn't mean it isn't on the black market. It's C-4 alright, and I've got six lab men who will stake their jobs on it. Will you do the same?"

McNeely backed off. "Hell. Okay, somebody could have brought it in from Jersey. You can buy any goddamned thing you want to over there in them swamps."

Mark had gotten close enough to hear the entire

exchange. He pulled at some wires in a mass of wreckage and made some notes on his pad, then began moving toward the exit. He'd heard enough, and it could provide him with that one slim thread that would lead back to the blasters and to Black Gold. Every big town he knew of had a spot where you could deal in outlawed guns, ammunition and explosives. He was sure New York would fit the pattern with at least one such outlet.

As he worked his way over to the stairs he moved slowly, stopping to examine wires. Then he went up the steps as quietly as he could. When he came to street level, a new cop prowled the site, which had now been barricaded. The cop waved, and Mark nodded as he walked past him toward the official limousines, then on to his own car. When the cop looked away, Mark got into the Continental and drove down Broadway. He found a parking space just off the main stem in the Sixties and chased down a telephone.

It took him two minutes to scramble through his memory and come up with the telephone number of the place in Los Angeles where he had done his weapons business. An operator placed his call from a pay phone and a minute later he had Sal Mitzuzaki on the wire. Mark identified himself with a few choice phrases in Japanese, then asked for a contact in New York where he could do some business. Sal hedged and said it was tough to be sure of identities on the phone. He gave Mark a double-safe address. He was to go to the bar there and ask for the Colonel. If the Colonel phoned for an I.D. check they would use a code based on Mark's appearance and what he had purchased last.

Mark thanked him and hung up. It was nearly four when he found the bar in the East Sixties and went inside. He nursed a beer and kept his ears open; but when nothing developed, he called the bartender and showed him the edge of a ten-dollar bill.

"I want to see the Colonel," Mark said.

"What for?"

"What the hell do you think for? Tell him I want to see him."

The barkeep was big, but not as big as Mark. The man rubbed his jaw a moment.

"You got to show some respect. The man's name is Colonel Borthwaite."

"Look boy, don't give me none of your damn lip. I want to see the Colonel. Now get your ass out of here and pass the word." Mark stared down the man. Just before he turned, the barkeep gave Mark a little grin.

Before Mark finished his beer, two men appeared and slid onto the bar stools on either side of him. In the mirror Mark saw that both were muscle men, but without the surly confidence of Mafia soldiers. When the first spoke his voice was higher than Mark expected.

"You looking for somebody?"

"I want to see the Colonel," Mark said, using the exact words Sal had told him to. Mark turned and stared at the man. He guessed he'd been a tackle, or maybe a guard. It was hard to tell now. The man shrugged.

"Come on," the ex-jock said, and slid off the stool.

They went into a back room just behind the bar.

The man with the high voice turned and held up his hands, palms out.

"No trouble, right? You heeled?"

Mark nodded.

"You got to give me your iron. Nobody sees the Colonel with a piece on him."

Mark shrugged. "Reasonable." Mark gave him the .22 and the other man hefted it.

"Nice balance. Anything else?"

Mace shook his head and a man behind him frisked him quickly, expertly. Mark was sure that that one had been a cop at one time. They led him through another door, down a hall and into a lavishly furnished room. Soft music pulsated from several unseen speakers. A thick shag rug covered the floor. It was a den, a man's *macho* room. On one paneled wall hung an elk's head with one antler prong missing. Behind a big, expensive desk sat a small man, with an oversized head much too large for his small body.

Tiny black eyes nailed Mark as soon as he came in and checked him expertly.

"Name?"

"Hanson, from L.A." He had to use that name, which was the one Sal Mitzuzaki knew him by.

"Who told you to see me?"

"Are you the Colonel?"

Anger began to show in the man's large face. Mark didn't react. At last the head nodded.

"The little Jap, Sal Mitzuzaki, in Los Angeles."

The Colonel looked up quickly. "Let's see your driver's license."

"No. Not unless you want to take it away from

me, and you'll need more than these two funny-farm jocks to do it."

The Colonel's black eyes drilled into Mark again; then he picked up a phone. He consulted a small book, then dialed direct. Identification was always done by phone; the strange little man had been testing him.

Mark sat down and looked at a *Playboy* magazine as the man talked. Two minutes later the Colonel hung up the phone.

The large head looked at Mark. "You may not know our procedures. You seem to check out, but we don't take any chances. You'll be blindfolded and taken to our warehouse. After your business is done, you'll be blindfolded again and brought back here. Then you can collect your weapon and leave through the bar."

Mark stood. "Hell, that's fine with me. I deal with insecure people all the time." The small man bristled.

The car ride was not short, but Mark had no way of knowing if they were going on a direct route or if they were trying to confuse him. He didn't try to trace the direction; he leaned back and relaxed. When they stopped he was helped out of the car and taken into a building. They then took his blindfold off and continued down iron stairs to a basement. It was dark except for a few key lights. At the far end he found the man who ran things. He was of average size, bald, with mod metal-rimmed glasses holding chunks of plate glass an inch thick over his eyes.

"Ah, yes, Mr. Hanson. Sal says you're okay, even if you are a little square. He keeps worrying that you might be mixed up in something legitimate or laudatory."

Mark automatically evaluated the man. A third-stringer, definitely a supervisor type. The Colonel ran the show, this one was just a hired hand.

"Sal talks too damn much," Mark said.

The bald man laughed. "All of us salesmen talk too much. What's on your mind?"

"You got any good C-4? Some good stuff, not any of that sweaty outdated touchy junk."

"You get fussy, son, and I'll send you out to Du Pont. We got C-4; you want it, you take what we give. Nobody seems to be complaining about quality. Fact is I moved over a hundred and fifty pounds last month. No problems at all."

"Did it go to Harlem?"

"I couldn't say. Why?"

" 'Cause some damn niggers up there just blasted one of my operations, and they used C-4. I'm gonna burn them good. I want the name and address where you delivered that C-4."

The man stood behind the old desk and shook his head. "You know this business better than that, Hanson. We never give out names. If Sal hadn't said nice things about you, that crack could get you clubbed and thrown into the river. No way I'm gonna tell you where that C-4 went."

"You must not have talked to Sal very long, buddy, or he would have told you that when I want something I get it. Now, come across with those goddamned names!"

The bald man laughed. "Hanson, you're forgetting the two men just behind you. They're my best boys." As he talked the man came around his desk. Mark saw the bulge under the right arm. He was a lefty, that was fine. As the man came up to Mark he was still talking.

"Now, if you want to buy some goods, to do in some blacks, that's fine with us."

The two men were still behind him, relaxed, not expecting trouble. Mark tensed, gathering his powers. His hand came up in a "what's-the-use" gesture, and at the same time he jumped backwards, slashing out his right foot, smashing it just over the belt line of the nearest jock, ramming it hard into the man's kidney. As Mark dropped quickly to the ground he recovered and saw the supervisor digging for his weapon.

Mark sprang forward from a crouch in one smooth movement, slamming his right forearm across the chest of the second guard before he knew what was happening. Jock number two dropped from the heart blow and fell beside his buddy, writhing on the cement floor. Mark reversed his field so quickly that Baldy didn't have time to pull his weapon out of the leather. He probably hadn't drawn it in years.

Mark slapped at his face, ripping the glasses off and bounching them onto the desk. He grabbed Baldy's arm, twisting it behind his back. Mark discarded the arm and wrapped his right arm around Baldy's throat from behind. He lifted the weapon, a .38, from his victim.

"Stay down, both of you," Mark snapped at the men on the floor. "Hands on top of your heads, lace the fingers. NOW!"

Dragging Baldy with him, Mark cautiously pulled .45's from both the guards, snapped out the magazines, and made sure the chambers were clear, then threw the weapons down an aisle. He grabbed the nearly blind Baldy and pushed him down into the desk chair.

"The name and address, Baldy. Get it now!"

"You don't keep records like that."

Mark jammed the .38 hard into the soft underside of Baldy's chin. The man yelped in pain.

"You want a neat round hole starting there and coming out the top of your skin head?"

"No. . . . please no!"

"Get the name."

Mark watched him pulling out drawers, fumbling at the bottom of one for a thin sheet of paper. The two jocks on the floor were still in pain. One groaned and pulled up his legs to lessen his kidney pain.

"If you didn't know Sal, you'd be one dead man by now, Baldy. Don't push me. Just get the address and quit trying to play it tough. You're a lightweight. Sal will tell you how to live to an old age in this business. You're outclassed, Baldy. Ninety-five percent of your customers could turn you and your goons inside out with one hand." He let a note of tiredness, of disdain creep into his voice. It made Baldy straighten up fast.

"My glasses?"

He opened the folded paper. On the next to last line on the bottom of the page he pointed to a name. Mr. Black, 132nd Street, The Daley Auto Painting Company. Mark glanced at it, memorized the line instantly, and stepped away from the desk.

"On your feet, boys. Then get those hands back on top. Who has the car keys?"

Mark marched all three men up the iron stairs. One jock had trouble walking because of his kidney kick, but he made it. At the outside door Mark stopped them.

"Baldy, as they say in sports, no harm, no foul. I haven't harmed you, or hurt your operation here."

"Just my glasses, they're bent . . ."

"You're lucky. I needed information and that's all I took, right? You try to get me in trouble with Sal and I'll fly back here and C-4 this joint into the Atlantic Ocean. You hear me good? And don't get smart and try to call the Colonel or this auto painting outfit. This little party is just with Mr. Black and me. I won't even mention this to the Colonel, which should get you off the hook. Give the boys here fifty bucks each and they'll forget it ever happened. Right, men?"

They both bobbed heads.

"Yeah, yeah," Baldy said slowly. "I got it. No sweat. No harm, no foul. You didn't want to buy what we had." He blinked several times and tried to focus on Mark. "Hell, okay, one of the guys can drive you back to the bar."

Mark kept the .38 during the car trip. Inside the back room of the bar they gave him his Hi-Standard pistol and he took the slugs out of the .38 and gave it back to the driver. His .22 was still loaded. Mark went through the bar and out the front door before anybody changed his mind.

Mark walked to his car and opened the door, then went back and gave the newsboy on the corner a dollar for watching his rig. He slid in and turned on the big engine. It gunned into action eagerly and he reached for the shift lever.

At that moment a cold, metallic object nuzzled into the back of his neck. He froze. Mark knew it was

43

a gun muzzle, and his own iron was buried in his hip leather a million miles away. There was nothing he could do. He didn't have a chance of reaching his weapon in time.

4

IT FIGURES 36-24-37

"Just relax, big man. Sit very still and keep both hands on the steering wheel."

Mark swore. It was a woman's voice, and it had the ring of competence. The gun in his neck was precisely placed; he was helpless. He began to turn and the gun jammed harder.

"No. Don't move," she said.

"A robbery like this takes lots of guts, lady."

"I'm not robbing you, all I want is some information. You just came out of the bar. Before that you vanished from inside and were gone more than an hour."

"You a cop?"

"No, I'm not a cop. Did you talk to the Colonel, and did you get to the warehouse?"

"Look, I don't know what the hell you're talking about. If you're not a cop and not some female Jesse James, put down the damn gun. Then we can talk."

She laughed lightly and he liked the sound of it.

"We'll talk this way. Did you get to the warehouse?"

"Look, lady. I know you aren't going to shoot off my head, 'cause then I couldn't answer any questions. So I'm going to turn around and look at you. Then maybe we can talk. Just go easy on that trigger, because I'm turning."

He did, and felt the pressure ease on the weapon. As he came around in the seat he saw a flash of silver blonde hair and a pretty face with a frown distorting the perfection of her clear skin and excellent makeup. She looked like a model, with high cheekbones, wide-set hazel eyes, and a nose that was perfect Elizabeth Taylor modern.

"Satisfied?" she asked.

"Just a quick inventory. I always like to see the person who is threatening to blast me into eternity."

"Now you know." She smiled and he felt a strange stirring. "Did you talk to the Colonel? I heard you ask the bartender to see him. Then the two big enforcers came out and you went into the back room with them. That's the only part of it I know."

"Lady, if you're not a cop, why the hell are you so interested in the Colonel?" He stared at her critically. She was the prettiest girl he'd seen in a long time. She wore a bright red pants suit and a white blouse with frilly cuffs and collar. He guessed she was about twenty-five.

"It doesn't really matter what I am. I have the gun. I'm gathering evidence against the Colonel and his illegal operations. I could be a private detective, or just a concerned citizen. It really doesn't matter. I know you saw the Colonel and I want some information."

46

She stared at him as she said it. He met her eyes and frowned. For just a fraction of a second she couldn't match his gaze and she glanced away. As she did Mark surged up and across the back seat, grabbing her gun hand and twisting the small automatic away from her. He stopped halfway into the back seat, his head landing in her lap. He looked up past her full breasts at her surprised and angry face.

"Damn it," she said softly.

He pushed away and saw a tear forming in her eye. Quickly he got out of the car and into the back seat beside her. She hadn't moved since he took her gun. The tears overflowed and crawled down a soft cheek. She blinked, then brushed back a strand of silver hair. He watched her. There was some magic quality about her, something so deeply appealing that it caught Mark by surprise. Only one other woman had ever affected him this way.

His voice was gentle when he spoke. "Now, why don't we start this whole thing over. It hasn't gone very well. My name is Henry Joerden. I'm here from Los Angeles on a case and I rented this buggy, so let's not shoot it full of holes."

She wiped her eyes and took a long slow breath.

"Damn it, Henry, I guess you win this round. I'm Joanna Tabler. I don't believe you're a cop, and I'm simply furious at myself because you took my gun away from me. I even had it on safety so I couldn't accidentally shoot anybody."

"That's no way to kill people."

"I wasn't going to kill you."

"I knew that, which is why it was easy to get your weapon."

He opened his billfold and showed her his private

detective's license and gun permit from San Bernardino.

"Well, I was wrong again. So far that's a zero batting average for two times up. Now can I get out of here and go paste myself back together again?"

Mark stared at the clinging suit top, the tight waist and the trim legs. "Joanna, from here it looks like your body is already very well pasted together."

A brief smile flashed through her despair.

"Now, Joanna, why are you interested in the Colonel? Are you F.B.I., or the C.I.A.?"

Her big hazel eyes stared straight into his. "No, I work with a lawyer and we know that this man is selling illegal arms. One of our clients was machine-gunned and is paralyzed. If we can prove the defendant got the weapon from the Colonel, we can prove ownership and possession, which should about wrap up the case for us. Now, please, Henry. Did you get into the warehouse?"

He leaned in toward her, caught the light scent of perfume and hesitated just a moment to let her back away. The he kissed her lips softly. She didn't respond.

"Henry, did you get into that downtown warehouse?"

"Can't say. It's a confidential matter."

He kissed her again, this time sliding his arm around her shoulders, pulling her close to him. She relaxed for just a moment, then pushed away.

"Now stop that. How do you expect me to think clearly . . ." She took a long breath and moved to the far side of the seat.

"Don't you see, Henry? I've simply got to nail this guy."

48

He smiled. "Sure you do. So you watched me go into the back room. You went outside and asked the newsboy which car he saw me park. Then you picked the lock and waited inside my car. You've just an innocent little legal secretary trying to help out her boss on her lunch hour."

She grinned and looked up at him with intense hazel eyes. "Does that sound a little weak?"

"Ridiculously weak."

"All right, so I was lying. I still need to know where the Colonel's warehouse is. That's all, Henry, just a street address." She smiled. "Please, Henry, let's make a deal, let's work together on this one."

He was tempted. If he closed his eyes it almost seemed as though he were listening to Donna. He brushed back his black moustache and shook his head.

"Can't do it, Joanna. We work for different clients. Can I drop you off somewhere, take you to dinner? Invite you up to my room? Fly with you to Paris?"

She laughed and shook her head. Then her face changed and became serious. She sighed.

"My car is just down the street. But at least you can tell me where you're staying. If you don't I'll check with airport rentals and get your address."

Mark got out of the back seat as she climbed out on the far side.

"So check," he said.

She stared at him over the roofline.

"Not even a clue?"

"Hell no. You're a beautiful, sexy, smart lady cop. That means you can find your own clues." Mark stepped into the front seat and drove off. He knew she would take his license plate number and phone the rental agency. It would give her something to do.

He drove back to the Algonquin, put the car into the parking valet's careless hands and went up to his room. His map of New York City put 132nd Street right in the middle of Harlem. It wasn't the most healthy place for a white man to go snooping around, as John Washington had reminded him. And yet, he wanted to make a soft recon on the site without drawing any enemy fire, or even letting their G-2 know he was there. Mark stared out the window, then phoned a theatrical supply store.

An hour later he came back to the Algonquin in a cab with a sack of supplies. He worked for two more hours in his room perfecting the technique. At last he developed just the right chocolate brown coloring to go on his hands, arms and face. It would be a close enough black-man color to let him move around Harlem without a second glance.

By the time he was satisfied, it was too late to probe the auto painting store. It would be closed, and he wasn't ready for a hard attack. He wanted to see some of the people who worked there, perhaps the man who owned it, get a reading.

He made a trial run to the hotel dining room, testing out his makeup, talking to waiters, bellhops. No one seemed to suspect that he wasn't a real black. After the meal he walked down Broadway along the Great White Way, the sin-town section. There he watched the movements and listened to the chatter of the blacks. He was refining, updating his "black" mannerisms.

Later, from his room, he telephoned Professor

Haskins at the Stronghold in California and brought him up to date on the mission. The professor agreed that he should move into an action operation. He gave Mark two more names to contact, one of a detective who had worked the Columbia University area fifteen years ago, and another of a Chinese man who ran a business.

Mark bought all the daily newspapers and went over each story that touched on the bombing and the radio proclamation. He found little that was new, but did see the exact wording of the bombing threat. He clipped each story and put them all in an envelope in his suitcase.

Mark checked his face in the mirror. He could have used some rings in his nostrils to flare them, and a little cotton padding in his cheeks. But he decided he wouldn't need the disguise for that long, nor would it be that difficult. All he had to do was get inside the painting firm and fool a couple of people for a few minutes.

He tried to call Lee Wong, the Chinese man the professor had talked about, but the firm was closed. At the 59th precinct they told him the detective he asked about had retired almost ten years ago.

Mark got up at six the next morning, checked his blackface and found it had stained his pillow. He rejuvenated it until he was sure he could pass, then had breakfast in a little grill on Broadway. He drove into Harlem and found 132nd Street and the big building with the sign: Daley Auto Painting. It was not doing a rushing business, but at least it was open. He parked near it and went in the door marked "office."

A thin Negro girl with big glasses sat at a desk working on some books. She looked up and kept right on chewing a mouth full of gum.

"Yeah?"

"Got some wheels, mama. Need some paint."

She grinned. "No lie?" She looked outside and saw the new Continental and frowned. "You jivin' me man? That's a new biscuit you got there."

"True, mama, but it's the wrong color."

"Oh."

"How much?"

She gave him four prices. He nodded. "Sounds good, mama. How about letting me look over your layout? Never been inside a painting outfit."

The girl shook her head. He figured she must be about eighteen. She was so flat-chested her padded bra provided the only bumps in her blouse.

"No way. Our insurance don't let nobody in there. You go and get yourself kilt, man, you cause us a pot of trouble." She was grinning as she said it.

"Now, come on, mama. I got to look over the place before I let you have my baby. Don't want you to ding me to death. I ain't gonna put my new wheels in a bang and splash shop."

She frowned, and backed up a step. "Now I *know* you jivin' me. You the heat?"

"What?"

She pushed a buzzer on the desk. When Mark looked up he saw a heavy-set black man coming through the side door. He looked at the girl.

"Throw this bitchin' motherfucker outa here, Lou," the girl yelled.

Lou wore a ripped, paint-splotched T-shirt and Levis. He took two steps toward Mark, then slid

52

something from his pocket. With a flip of his wrist a five-inch blade snapped out and locked into place. The steel glinted in the morning sunlight. He held the weapon low.

"You going out easy, man?" Lou asked.

Mark judged him quickly. Over six feet but soft. Probably had some early success with a knife to build his confidence, but no military hand-to-hand training. Too cocky. Mark stood waiting, his shoulders dropped.

"Now, look, man, I just want a paint job. I ain't looking for no trouble, sure as hell no blade!" He stepped back a foot and Lou kept coming forward. The change in position broke the timing of the black man.

Lou slowed, circled to the left. They were four feet apart, the knife low, ready, deadly. Mark started a right-hand chop toward the knife arm. The blade slashed upwards toward his hand, then changed direction as Lou lunged forward, the steel aimed at Mark's belly. Mark's left hand swung down hard and Lou yelped as the chop cracked into his forearm.

Lou recovered and danced back, cautious, more respectful. Mark advanced on him, faked a chop against the knife hand, faked a driving finger-stab with his other hand; then, when Lou quickly countered for both, Mark drove forward a step and kicked hard. Lou was wide open in a feet-apart defending stance.

Mark's heavy boot skidded off Lou's thigh, then drove upward, smashing into his scrotum, blasting his balls up against his pelvic bones. One of the testes smashed, hemorrhaging. Lou dropped to the floor screaming hysterically, a mass of twisted, thrashing arms and legs.

The girl ran. Mark vaulted a low desk and caught her a yard from the back door. He dragged her with him back to Lou.

"You scream, little mama, and I'll rip this wing right off your shoulder, dig?"

She did.

Mark bent and tore the T-shirt off Lou's chest. Lou moaned and writhed on the floor, first holding his genitals, then groaning at the touch.

Mark picked up the fallen knife and carved a thin line down the center of the black chest an eighth of an inch deep, letting the red blood flow, filling the furrow, spilling out on the dark skin. A second line went across the top of the first, forming a T. Blood pooled, slanted off the body and dripped on the floor. Mark lay the blade on the floor and put his foot on it, then pulled upward sharply on the handle, snapping off the blade.

"Never pull a knife on me again, Lou, or I'll kill you."

He dragged the girl behind him toward the door she had run for. "Where does this lead?"

"Backshop."

"Anybody there?"

"Yeah, Joe and some new cat."

"We're going to take a look. You walk ahead and go where I say. Don't jive me about those other guys or you gonna lose that padded bra and blouse of yours. Dig?"

She nodded, hatred building in her eyes.

It was a bump and sand backshop, with two men working on a battered Cadillac with pneumatic hammers, creating a continuous yammering of metal on metal. Neither man looked up as they walked by. The tour continued into another section of the building, containing offices and one larger area that looked like it had been set up as a meeting room. They saw no other people.

"There's nothing here, dammit!" the black girl said. "What the hell you think you're looking for?"

He ignored the question, pushing her ahead of him down a short hall to another room. It was a wildly overdecorated woman's boudoir. No one was there, just a large round bed and a dozen pillows. They went back to the hall, and had started down it when the black girl jerked loose from his grasp and dove sideways to the floor.

"Shoot, Soo Lin. Shoot him!" the black girl screamed.

The sound came from behind, a high-pitched snarl of a .22 hand gun with a deadly sting.

5

MR. MAYOR'S PAYOFF

Mark felt the slap of air against his face as the small slug whipped past. Even before the booming sound of the shot had reached its peak, Mark dove to his left, away from the weapon and toward the black girl. He came up behind her and pulled the slender girl across his body.

Now he had a second to look at the attacker. She stood twenty feet down the hall, a pistol gripped in both hands. She was Chinese, and the black girl had called her Soo Lin. She could be the same one Mr. Washington had talked about.

The Chinese girl hesitated.

'Shoot, goddammit!" Mark's shield screamed. "Kill the sonafabitch. Don't worry about me!"

Mark swept his Colt Commander from his hip leather and shot into the wall beside Soo Lin. She yelped and darted into a doorway.

He picked up the black girl with one arm and carried her in front of him as he backed away down the hall. He found another door and opened it. Stairs led down to what he hoped would be an outside exit.

Just as he started down, a tall black man ran to the foot of the steps and a heavy shot whistled past Mark. The reliable Commander responded to his kill-or-be-killed motivation and a big .45 slug slammed into the black man's head, jolting him backwards, splattering the wall with blood and brains. The girl screamed and began sobbing. He tossed her over his shoulder and carried her down the stairs. Mark dropped a blue flint arrowhead on the corpse and pulled open the door a crack. He was back at the body shop. Just across the big room he saw that the truck entrance doors had been rolled open.

Mark pushed the girl to the floor and sprinted into the shop, past the two men still working on the Cadillac and out the big truck doors. The body men didn't even look up.

He ran to the Continental and leaped inside. But as he left the small lot, he drove cautiously, trying not to attract any special attention. Mark saw no one come out the doors of the paint shop behind him.

He wondered about it as he drove downtown. It had been a violent and unexpected reaction. What were they so touchy about? At first he was only a prospective customer with some questions. For that a goon had threatened him with a knife. Then he had been viciously attacked. He was shot at by the Chinese girl and finally by a man also trying to kill him. He would watch closely to see if the death was reported in the newspapers. If it wasn't, it could mean he had the first small handle on Black Gold.

And if that Chinese witch was the same Soo Lin, he might have a positive lead.

Lt. Larry Butler hated these damned meetings. His Honor the Mayor of New York City had called it, and while Larry didn't hobnob with the mayor that often, he knew how it would turn out. He wiped one hand back through his thinning brown hair and checked around the table.

The mayor sat at the end in a big leather chair. He had ice water and 7-Up beside him, and another large 7-Up bottle which everyone knew contained Beefeater's gin. Next to him sat Reilly, a smart-assed, snot-nosed kid lawyer and the mayor's executive assistant. Reilly wasn't half dry behind the ears yet, and he was an arrogant bastard besides. Then came the boss, Police Commissioner McNeely, old and slobby with 280 pounds of beer belly, but only six months in some jerkwater police department in Jersey before he got this appointment. He had something on the mayor, that was for damn sure. McNeely kept talking.

"Mr. Mayor, I don't give a rat's ass what them black sons of bitches say. There is no way you can win by buying off a blackmailer. You try it and he hits you again and ups the ante. Let my boys run them down. So they blow one more station, we'll be ready for them this time."

The mayor grimaced sadly. "Randy, how many key target subway stations would you say we have in Manhattan alone?

"We figure forty."

"And you're going to guard forty stations around

the clock, for two weeks, two months, even two years?"

"Yes, sir. We can do it. We have the men . . ."

"Commissioner, that's ridiculous," Reilly broke in with his Harvard accent and his condescending tone. "Do you realize how much it's costing the city to repair and rebuild that one small station? Over three million dollars, and the estimates are not even all in yet. Another station would be just as much, and what if they hit Grand Central? It could cost a billion if some of the main supports on buildings were affected. And think what it could cost in lost business! Gentlemen, remember the mayor's special committee has recommended that we pay the money."

Lt. Butler couldn't keep quiet any longer. He hated to agree with the commissioner on anything, but this time he had to.

"Mr. Mayor, I've handled a few blackmail cases in twenty-one years on the force. It never works. You can't satisfy that easy-money syndrome. Pay them once and you'll be paying them every month for life. The only way to deal with blackmail and hijacking is to refuse to cooperate, to blast them, to run them down, drive them into the open and burn them. You let one punk outfit like this hijack you and you'll attract half the easy-money experts from all over the world. The damn Arabs will be here next, and the bomb will be in your office."

"Butler, that's a scare tactic," Reilly snapped.

"Young man, I'd rather scare you than have to pick up your mangled, blown-apart body some day," Lt. Butler said.

The mayor held up his hand. "Bickering won't get

us anywhere. My special committee did suggest we pay. But as they arrive to collect, we close our dragnet so tightly they can't get out. Then we use them for bait to trap the rest of the gang."

Danny Aaron took the floor. Butler remembered him as the man in charge of streets and traffic control.

"Have any of you driven past 72nd Street today?" Aaron asked. "It's virtually impossible, even with alternate routes, twice as many surface buses and an appeal for car pools. If they hit three more stations we might as well close up shop and go fishing. I say we pay them now, stall any more bombings and catch them at the payoff."

Someone else began talking. There were twelve men around the big mahogany table, and Larry was sure that each one would take his turn. Larry tuned out the man talking, letting the signal come across as a low mumble. He was thinking about his cabin at the lake. He'd been very careful about living on his police salary. Nobody ever questioned him. Most detectives were on the take, and a lot got caught, but he was never suspected. The two hundred extra a month from the "club" he belonged to came under the heading of poker winnings, and not even his wife Martha knew any different. That money had paid for the cabin on the lake in Connecticut. He was looking forward to going up on his next two-day relief.

Larry shifted lower in his chair, looking up at the mayor, then around the room. It would be all over in an hour and he would be out of it. The chief and the commissioner would take over. The only reason he was at the meeting was because the bombing happened in his precinct when he was on duty. They would probably appoint two captains and maybe a SWAT team. He'd be out of it and off on that fishing trip.

Twenty minutes later the mayor made a decision. They would pretend to pay off the blackmailers, and then follow through and make damn certain the pickup man was caught. The mayor looked at Larry Butler.

"Commissioner, I want Lt. Butler to handle the payoff. He seems to have a good feel for these people. Use him as close to the actual payoff as you can."

The slow burn began in Lt. Butler's gut again, right next to a touch of panic.

"Thank you, Mr. Mayor," Larry said and knew that the panic would turn into numbness.

After that they broke up into separate meetings. One dealt with raising the money. They would get fifty thousand dollars in used twenty-dollar bills from each of forty banks.

Later, precisely at 1:50, they gathered in the police chief's office. The Black Gold man had said he would call promptly at 2 p.m. Butler, Chief of Police Dan Perkins, the commissioner and half a dozen others waited for the call. A lot depended on how this went. If they could keep the man on the phone for about three minutes, the call could be traced. They hoped to get started right by catching the gang member who placed the call.

When the phone rang, the police tape recorder went on; then the commissioner took the call.

"Hello, this is Commissioner McNeely."

"Yeah, baby, who else?"

61

"Who is this?"

There was a low laugh. "Yeah, Commish, you'd shit in a basket to find that out, wouldn't you? This is Black Gold, white man, so hang onto your hats. I'm gonna give you the straight word how you honkey bastards gonna cough up some loot to keep your white damn town open. You dig?"

"Yes, I understand. We're ready and willing. Where do we bring the money?"

"You just listen. When I want to hear your fat-assed voice I'll ask you. Got that?"

"Yes."

Signals were being waved in the chief's office indicating that the telephone trace was well under way. The chief put the call on his telephone desk speaker so they all could hear.

"Now, Commish, baby. This is how we'll work it. First I don't want no cop car. You get yourself a 1963 Chevy, a two-door. Want you to have a sweet little soul sister, some black woman cop, to drive the car. Now, don't hide no fuzz inside the car or your Uncle Tom girl will be in a box full of trouble.

"You have her drive the Chevy down Flatbush Avenue into Brooklyn. You'll be notified after she starts driving where she should stop. I'll phone you. Be sure she takes a police walkie-talkie radio in her car, but fix it so it will receive only, and not transmit. That way she won't be tempted to get herself shot. When she crosses into Brooklyn we'll let you know where to stop. You better get this all down, man, cause I ain't gonna repeat it.

"Soon as she gets to her stop in Brooklyn she'll have instructions what to do. Remember, you damn honkey cops, no tails, no following her, and no chop-

62

pers. You do and your little black chippie is gonna be turkey meat fast.

"You have that good loot in used twenties, *used* ones. And don't worry trying to copy down all them serial numbers, there ain't time enough!"

Frantic signalling in the office indicated the trace was complete; they had a phone booth in Harlem pinpointed as the source of this call. Immediate radio calls went out for prowl cars in the area to converge on the booth and to take the man alive.

The speaker on the desk droned on:

"Well, man, you honkey kiss-ass cops, looks like that's about it. Next time you hear from me, I'll be a millionaire. How about that. Sure hope you had the phone call traced. Your boys good with booby traps? Just a suggestion, know what I mean, man?"

The speaker quieted; only a soft hum came through.

"Are you still there?" the commissioner asked. "Hello? Hello?"

There was no response so the commissioner hung up the phone. "Well, I guess that's it," he said.

One minute after the voice stopped on the loudspeaker, the radio came through with a message. The phone booth had been spotted, but there was no one in it.

"Be careful, he said something about a booby trap," Police Chief Perkins told them.

They took the booth, captured it. The only thing it contained was one cheap tape recorder with a played-out casette. The bomb squad arrived and checked the recorder. It looked harmless enough. A thin probe under one corner lifted it but they saw nothing under it. Carefully they put an open-bottom bomb basket over the recorder and tried to slide the steel bottom cover plate under the recorder, to trap it inside the blast-proof container. The probe hit something. At last they lifted it anyway.

The officer who died in the instant blast never knew why. A half pound of C-4 had been pressed in place under the telephone-booth shelf where the recorder sat. A thin steel push-rod held down the bomb trigger. As long as the tape recorder kept pushing it down, the C-4 would not detonate. The instant the recorder was lifted the bomb went off. Ten officers were injured, one patrol car set on fire, and one valuable piece of evidence destroyed.

A half a block away, from the top of a two-story building, Abdul Daley watched the whole scene through 8 x 30 binoculars. When the blast went, he grinned and faded across the building toward the fire escape.

An hour later the Chief's investigation was over. The phone booth was near a warehouse. No one had seen anybody enter or leave the area all day.

During that same hour squad cars all over the city searched for a 1963 Chevy two-door. At last they spotted one in a Brooklyn used-car lot and hustled it into town. The black policewoman was no problem. She volunteered. She was Lt. Willa Johnson, 28, single, a crack shot, possessor of a brown belt in Karate and an M.S. degree in law enforcement.

The money came packed in two soft brown suitcases, and Lt. Butler stowed it in the back seat of the Chevrolet. A second phone call had instructed the Chevy to leave police headquarters promptly at 3 p.m.

Lt. Johnson got the rig underway on the dot and worked it down to Canal Street, then across the Manhattan Bridge into Brooklyn. She was two blocks from Prospect Park when the orders came through on her radio.

"Special Car 1963, Lt. Johnson. Proceed to west entrance Prospect Park. Under first trash can to your left inside park is message. It will give further instructions."

Lt. Larry Butler monitored the radio message on his hand-held set and grimaced. He used the radio to tell the forty patrol units alerted in Brooklyn to sit tight at their designated spots. He had been afraid of this kind of treasure hunt, meaning a moving target. Larry drove his private car, so there could be no easy I.D. on it. He wore his sports coat and slacks as usual. Now he juggled his forces in his mind, wondering just when to deploy them. Not yet, he decided. He called the choppers up to within a mile of the park on each side, and waited.

Larry parked near the exit of Prospect Park and watched. When the 1963 Chevy drove out, he watched carefully, but could see no other car move out to follow it. He waited there as long as he could without losing the Chevy.

Larry drove well back, keeping a visual contact with the Chevy, letting other cars drift between them but never losing sight, staying in the same lane. There was no doubt in his mind that they would catch the blackmailers. He had the entire police force of New York City at his disposal. The choppers were now starting to shadow his car from a mile back. He had painted a big white number "8" on the top of his black sedan. He could call on two hundred prowl cars if he needed them. The pickup man didn't have a chance.

As he thought it through he realized the Chevy ahead of him was angling toward Kennedy International Airport. Soon they were on the Southern Parkway; they drove under the Van Wyck Expressway, past the big airfield, and out along the multi-laned road at sixty miles an hour.

The first hint of panic hit him when he saw the sign showing the turnoff for the town of Valley Stream two miles ahead. In a few minutes they would be outside of the city, heading into Long Island. He hadn't even considered alerting the hundreds of small-town police departments on Long Island. It would be an impossible job. He was in hot pursuit, so he could legally make an arrest, but he couldn't call in his own reserves, his thousands of N.Y.P.D. officers.

When he radioed Chief Perkins to tell him where he was and about the potential problem, he heard the chief explode.

"Dammit, I knew something would go wrong. We're not dealing with a bunch of dummies. Radio Lt. Johnson and tell her to break off the delivery, to return to New York City jurisdiction at once."

Larry tried. He made six transmissions, but the car kept right on going. He told Chief Perkins.

"Goddamn."

"They probably made her leave the radio in the trash can in Prospect Park," Larry said. "Have a unit check that out."

Lt. Butler had been keeping the chief informed of where they were on the highway.

"I've alerted the state police to pick up her car

and hold it for us, or escort it back into our juris-diction," the Chief said a moment later. "I'm also spreading the word to every little town along that highway to watch for her and stop her. But you know those little villages, four cars and six men, probably won't do us a damn bit of good. It's going to be up to you, Butler, to close in and turn her around. Go now!"

"Yes sir."

He put down the radio and jammed the throttle to the floor. She was only a block ahead on a four-lane road. It would be simple. Twice he tried to pass the car just ahead of him, but both times he failed. They flashed through Valley Stream, and Larry tried again. Each time he came alongside the black 1974 Oldsmobile, it speeded up and angled toward him, cutting off his advance.

Exits showed for Rockville Center. Now he under-stood. The black Oldsmobile was deliberately keep-ing him behind so he could not stop Lt. Johnson. A short black man was driving it.

He fumbled for his .38, then saw there was no time. "Oh, God, if I lose her," he groaned.

He couldn't lose her. If he did he might just as well kiss that cabin goodbye, and his retirement . . .

Lt. Butler gripped the wheel tightly and charged toward the Oldsmobile. Again it veered toward him. He yelled and swung his wheel to the right, slam-ming his car into the Olds, bouncing it to the side and letting the faster Ford sheer past it with a screeching of body metal. He roared ahead and saw the blue Chevy turn onto the Wantagh off-ramp.

Butler whipped his car into the right-hand lane ahead of the Oldsmobile with a small thrill of victory. He slowed for the off-ramp turn, and in his mirror saw the Black Olds hurtling down on him. That was when Larry remembered he should have alerted the choppers to move in and track the blue Chevy. But it was too late. The idiot in the Olds was going too fast now. Larry speeded up, but the Olds smashed into the rear of his Ford, jetting it forward. The off-ramp curled sharply to the left as it climbed to overpass the super highway. The maximum exit speed was 25 mph. His Ford plowed into the turn at sixty. Larry fought the wheel, then felt the hard jolt as he crossed the low curb and smashed through the guard rail. He felt the car going airborne, shooting through the sky, curving downward, hitting the sloping landscaped bank and rolling.

It wasn't happening to him! Not after twenty-one years without even a smashed-in fender while on duty. From somewhere he smelled the rawness of gasoline. The damn tank had probably ruptured. He knew that only four out of one thousand cars in wrecks ever catch on fire. That was comforting. He was still rolling when the first trace of smoke reached him. The car took one last series of rolls and landed on its top in the middle of the highway, in the high-speed traffic lane. Now he could feel the heat.

Lt. Butler tried to open the seat belt that pinned him upside down in the smoke-filled car. His right hand didn't respond. He looked down and saw his arm dangling limply. He couldn't move it. His left shoulder hurt like hell too. As he lifted his left hand toward the belt release, fresh pain daggered through his shoulder and chest. But the hand was making it. Inch by inch he brought it up toward the damn release.

His hand was almost there when a skidding Datsun 240Z tried to change lanes too late and smashed into the right rear side of the battered Ford. Lt. Larry Butler's personal car made four complete spins on its roof, then crumpled to one side. A Dodge Charger couldn't avoid the moving target and made its last charge against the driver's side amidships. The impact slammed the car back onto its four flat tires, blocking both outside lanes.

Lt. Butler was still conscious. He couldn't move either hand now, or his head. He wondered why he wasn't dead. He decided right then that he wasn't going to waste his time by going on that fishing trip Monday. He wasn't even going to work!

Just then the gas tank exploded, converting the Ford into one large gasoline-fed funeral pyre. Before Lt. Butler drew his last breath in the searing flames, he laughed. Now nobody would ever be able to prove how he got that lakeside cabin in Connecticut.

6

COP ON THE ROCKS

Abdul Daley eased the battered black Oldsmobile to the side of the street and looked back at the off-ramp he had just left. He could see the gush of oily smoke lifting skyward near the overpass. That should be one less damn cop to worry about. He slid the damaged Olds forward, confident that the two-million-dollar Chevrolet would be stopped according to the plan.

The driver had been told to come off this ramp and pull in at the Shell station on the corner. Daley drove into the gasoline station just as the big roll-down door in front of the lube racks was being closed. He saw the flash of a blue Chevy and relaxed.

This wasn't the newest Shell station in the system. In fact this one had been in operation for almost forty years, and simply happened to be in the right location when the new highway went through. The lube rack room led into a much older building used as a garage, with ten service bays and a paint booth. Abdul parked the Olds just inside the second entrance to the garage. The Olds had been stolen an hour before the action that afternoon, and would be dumped later on. For now it was out of sight.

At the far end of the garage he saw the blue Chevy, which he had followed ever since it left police headquarters. He had spotted the cop in the civilian car which trailed the Chevy before he had gone a block. That one must have been a stupid pig cop not to figure out that there would be some kind of a follow-up car on the lady fuzz.

Abdul saw that the black bird was still inside the Chevy. She was one hell of a wild-looking chick. Yeah! He hoped she had the money and that everything was going according to plan. Be a shame to waste a pretty one like that. He paused behind the car and pulled a nylon stocking on over his head as a mask, distorting his features. Then he walked up to the car and opened the driver's door.

"I'll be damned, look at that, a black girl pig. Get out, oinker, and forget about your .38. We've got three guns aimed right at that great big beautiful chest of yours."

Lt. Willa Johnson hesitated. She had known she was in trouble as soon as they waved her car into the garage. Both Negro men had worn the nylon stocking masks. Both had had big .45's aimed right at her head. The station had been closed for regular business. Inside the building the choppers couldn't spot her from the air. She didn't have her radio, and she wasn't sure if anybody had followed her off the exit ramp or not. She twisted her mouth into a grimace. Yes, she had known the risks involved when she volunteered. Slowly she got out of the car, smoothing down the short skirt and satin blouse she had been wearing when the call for help came. There had been no time to go home and change.

"Well, well, well. We done caught ourselves a damn pretty bird," Abdul said. He walked around her, patted her tight little fanny. He grinned when she didn't gasp or yell or react in any way. "Yeah, and she's one smart mama, too. You did just fine, honey mama, bringing the loot just like we told you. Is it all there?"

"I didn't stop and count it," she said. "I assumed they put in what you asked for."

"How much was that, sweet mama?"

"You said two million on the radio."

Abdul laughed. Yeah, she was smart, and sexy as a two-hundred-dollar call girl. So she was eight inches taller than he was; he liked girls stacked tall sometimes.

Abdul reached in the back seat of the Chevy and took out the two suitcases. He put one down on the hood of the car and opened it. As he pushed up the lid the other three men in masks crowded around him and whistled.

"Goddamn, man, look at all that bread!"

"Sweet mutha, look at the long green."

As the men stared in wonder at all the money, Willa edged toward a door. A hand caught her wrist and jerked her back roughly.

"Sweet mama, you ain't going nowhere, not yet, and for sure not with all them clothes on." His hand caught one of her breasts through the blouse and she shivered.

72

Her foot came out viciously, aiming for his crotch, but Abdul shifted his position and her shoe glanced off the outside of his thigh. He slapped her. It came so fast she had no time to react. Instead she grabbed the hand still on her breast and held his wrist, pushing forward and down, bending the hand back until he started to lean backward and his knees buckled. She lifted her knee sharply, slamming it into his chest, dropping Abdul to the floor.

Two of the men jumped to take his place, and for a moment she thought one of the distorted faces looked Chinese. They came at her from both sides, and before she could use any of her karate, one man grabbed her from behind, squeezing her breasts until she screamed.

Lt. Johnson fought them every step of the way. Three of them carried her to an old couch at the side of the building. They held her legs and took off her shoes, then ripped off her skirt and cut it into ribbons and threw the pieces around. One used his knife and delicately cut the whole crotch out of her panty hose.

Abdul recovered from his chest blow and got there in time to rip off her blouse, tearing it into a dozen pieces. Then he jerked off her bra and cut it up with his knife.

Still they held her. Abdul looked down at her and laughed. She was good, a fine body, tiny waist, good slender legs, big breasts. One tall damn hunk of mama.

"Hold her," he growled at the two men, and took off his pants and went between her thighs.

Willa closed her eyes. She had known how it would end as soon as she tried to fight them. She

73

should have conned Abdul and gone with him to a motel, that would have been easier. Four of them. She shut her mind, and tried to turn off her nerves. She simply would not allow her body to feel anything, not a solitary thing.

Abdul lunged forward, stabbing inside her, and she screamed. A hand crushed down on her mouth.

Willa Johnson didn't try to keep track. They held her and took turns, trying to make her scream again. Gradually it all began to get hazy and fuzzy. She thought of laughing, but realized that she was sobbing instead. She tried to push up out of the deep, dense fog, but it kept washing over her, as everything became darker and darker, until finally there came total blackness. As she trailed off she wondered if this was what it was like to die. To drift into a long dreamless sleep. She didn't care. She welcomed the black oblivion.

When she woke, she found she was tied down. Willa had no idea how long she had been there. It was dark outside, but, strangely, it grew lighter in distinct stages, then suddenly turned dark again. She turned her head and saw a neon light blinking on with gradually increasing power, building up the light in the room, then turning off and recycling.

She frowned and stared at the room. It was a room! She was on a bed. It must be a motel room. They had moved her. A smelly rag gagged her mouth so she couldn't cry out for help. Her hands and feet had been tired to the four corners of the bed, spread-eagling her on her back. She was still naked. Willa let the tears come, streaming down her cheeks. They were tears of joy. At least she was still alive.

74

It had to be a motel room, and they probably put a "Do Not Disturb" sign on the door. It might be tomorrow afternoon before anyone found her. An overriding surge of panic threatened her; then she blinked back the tears, stopped shivering and tried to relax. Sleep, she should sleep. Gradually she whipped the panic. She was alive, she was not smashed up or slashed. She had to wait it out. Be calm, just relax.

Gradually sleep came to her, but she dreamed of men, hundreds of them, all with nylon stockings over their faces turning their features into those of weird, surrealistic madmen who kept tearing at her clothes.

Abdul Daley turned up the car's radio and pounded out a beat on the dash with both hands. He had been a drummer for a while, and pretty good. Then had come the trouble and the army, and the end of his sticks.

He had a stack of twenty-dollar bills in his hands and he kept riffling through them. Two hundred bills to a bundle, that was four thousand dollars. Two hundred and fifty packets in each suitcase made it a cool million dollars a bag. And it was all clean, no way it could be marked or traced, not all those used twenty-dollar bills.

Well, dammit, he had earned it! All those years of being pushed around, of being rousted by the damn cops, of doing time in the dumb-assed army, and getting spit on by the Panthers. It was time he started doing a little pushing of his own.

As the car droned along the highway back into Manhattan, he remembered the very first strike he had made. There were four of them, all about thirteen. They caught some old honkey who made a mistake and got out of the subway on Lenox Avenue, thinking he was on the Broadway train. They took him. Knocked him down so fast he never even saw them. They cleaned out his pockets, grabbed his watch and his two pens and his wallet, and were running down the street in thirty seconds. Twenty-two bucks they got for their trouble. Not bad for kids.

He was fifteen when he had his first knife fight. Hell, you weren't nothin' until you'd gone up against a blade in a real go. Had to draw blood too, and if the other jack landed in a hospital, you were a big man on the block for a month.

That was the year the pigs started bothering him. Tried to get him back to school, tried to get him to quit fighting. Then he caught a juvie rap for ninety days for beating up an old nigger who owed him money. After that the juvies were hot for his balls.

But he nailed one of them. He knew this one detective pig was on the take for a hundred a month from the numbers guy in that section of Harlem. This black pig detective was the first man Abdul ever killed. They argued about something, and Abdul threatened to tell a reporter about the numbers and the payoffs to all the detectives. The black cop panicked and came at Abdul with a knife. Ab flicked out his own six-inch switch blade. They danced around in the alley, and the cop sliced open Abdul's left arm. He was moving in to cut him again when Abdul took a wild swipe at the cop's face. He missed, but the blade bit into the detective's throat, slashing open his jugular vein. The man's blood and his life spewed out into the alley in a few seconds. Abdul took a hundred dollars off the body and planted some numbers slips on him. When the cop was found there was no publicity about it. The official report called it an accidental death, and nothing was mentioned about the numbers.

By the time Abdul was sixteen, he had been a member of the Black Panthers for nearly two years. He had a gun by then and could use it. He went to the meetings, helped set up two ambushes, and was in on a shootout that left two cops dead. Abdul was one of five Panthers brought to trial on that one, but after two hung juries, they were all freed.

When he was eighteen he finished his stint with the Panthers. They booted him out for being too militant, too bloodthirsty. The new thrust of the Panthers had shifted to political action rather than violence, and Abdul wanted none of it. He signed up for three years in the army just before he was to be drafted.

In the army he adapted with an effort, took the guff and the basic training just so he could use the weapons. He was a natural with all firearms, and soon the officers began to notice him. With hand weapons he often made the highest score of anyone in the entire training division.

He took a battery of tests and scored remarkably high in several categories, including mechanical aptitude and mechanical procedures. When his officers discovered he had gone to high school only half way through his sophomore year, they were amazed.

After basic he applied for training in explosives, booby traps, mines and delayed explosive devices.

He came out an expert sapper, qualified to handle all explosives and mines.

When he was satisfied that he knew all the army could teach him about weapons and explosives, he began a concentrated campaign for a discharge. In two months he had twelve Article 13 charges: late on passes, taking off without a pass, drunk in formation . . . In two more weeks he was out of the army on a "good of the service" discharge. It was exactly what he wanted and fit in perfectly with his plans.

Abdul went back to Harlem, where he began to set up his organization. He worked slowly, establishing a small core of expert burglars who worked for him. They built up a cash fund to use to buy a business for a front. By the time he was twenty-one he had the cash to buy an old auto painting firm. After that he moved into overdrive.

Black Gold was a secret organization for four years, building slowly, gaining new converts, establishing a treasure chest, making contacts, establishing operational procedures and picking targets.

Also during those four years he built a reputation for moving hard drugs. He gradually developed a special brand of pusher, and before long had a full-scale wholesale heroin trade functioning. He was never busted; he took care of the detectives on his district, and used the H to provide most of the revenue to finance other activites.

Now the big money was coming in. The city fathers had been a pushover. He should have tried this long ago. The cash was what he had to have. His organization had outstripped his regular money source. The only way Black Gold could grow now was with massive injections of hard cash. He had plans for political and action groups all over the nation; first in the large cities with heavy black populations, then in every big town.

When these units were in place and action-ready, he could make his move. Slowly he would gain a foothold in local governments; then, in paralyzing, slashing attacks, he would move in and take over key states. He would not need an army. An elite corps of assassins and terrorists can do the work of a panzer division and a score of atomic bombs, but more quickly and with less destruction.

Now he had the first piece of big money, and could start turning those plans into fact.

Abdul looked over at the man driving the car. He was Chinese, and the major reason Abdul had such a constant source of high-quality heroin. He had been working with the mainland Chinese for over four years. He had started slowly, cautiously, letting confidence grow on both sides. Now Soo Lin had come in as a special representative of her supplier. It was definitely a two-way street. They furnished him with the H, and he paid them. Then they did what they could for him in the way of help with organization, local support, special munitions and tactics training.

Soo Lin herself had been the sweetest part of the deal. He was surprised at what she would do with her body to delight him. She seemed to have an unending variety of ways to make love. Anything that was physically possible was fine with her. Abdul suspected she had other talents as well, but so far she had not demonstrated them. He knew she was a weapons and hit-and-run warfare expert. But he suspected she was at least a captain in the Chinese People's Secret Service. He never asked her. He would use these Chinese for as long as he needed them, then dispose of them in the East River some dark night, minus their hands and heads.

The car moved across the bridge into Manhattan, and Abdul eased back in the seat. He smoothed back the long duck's ass haircut and sighed. He liked the greased-down hair styles of the fifties. None of his people were allowed to wear an Afro haircut. He said they were degrading, harking back to the primitive savages of Africa. He was not a primitive, he was a modernist, and none of his Black Gold people could be mixed up with any of that old-fashioned jazz.

Later, when the car rolled into the Daley Auto Painting shop and the big door closed, Abdul let out a long screech of victory.

He had won!

A dozen anxious faces stared at him.

He jumped out of the car waving a stack of bills. "Brothers, sisters, we done won the whole pot. We have overcome. We got the damn two million dollars!"

There were whoops and yelps of joy, screams of delight. He ordered a banquet prepared and had six special girls brought in.

Soo Lin rushed up and kissed his cheek.

"I want to count all of it!" she squealed.

He caught her hand and led her away, making sure he had all the money with him. He spread the cash out on the bed.

"Beautiful, so damn beautiful!" he said.

He began to pull off Soo Lin's clothes.

"I've got some bad news, Abdul. A man was here today. He started shooting and got away. He was black. I don't know who he was, or what he wanted. He killed a man."

"Don't worry about it, we on the way now. Two million bucks!"

"I am worried. I hope he wasn't this freelance agent who has been shooting up Washington. They call him the Penetrator."

He kissed her and ripped off her blouse and pushed her back down on the bed on top of the money.

About midnight she woke him up.

"I forgot the good news. Chang got here today. Pao Lin Chang, my man from Hong Kong."

Abdul sat up blinking, and forced his eyes open. His fingers laced and his thumbs rubbed each other in slow, constant motion.

"So did he bring the stuff? Did he get in with it?"

"Yes, he's sleeping now. He said there was no trouble with his 'chemicals.' He said they were photochemicals. He was impressed at how stupid and lazy your customs inspectors are. He flew into Toronto, stayed overnight, then met some friends who drove him across the border. No problems. He said he was a student at City College here in New York and was born in San Francisco. They did not even open his suitcases."

"Yeah, we're pushovers. When's he gonna put the goop together, you know, activate it or whatever the hell he does? What did he call the stuff?"

"It's X-447."

"Yeah, wild. And will it do what you said it would?"

"We really don't know. It's never had a large-scale test like this. But we think it will."

"Well, baby Chink, we might just do a job with it. Oh, we'll give them plenty of time to pay up."

She smiled at him and rubbed his black, hairless chest.

"Darling, if we do use it, you and I, we must be far, far away."

"Oh, hell yes, no sweat about that, mama. It's some new kind of nerve gas, right? And your boy Chang got it in from Hong Kong?"

"Yes, darling, but it's not a nerve gas, it's a culture; a kind of fast-multiplying virus that is deadly to humans. It's extremely tough to counteract, and very long-lived. By using it right we can wipe out half the population of Manhattan in twenty-four hours."

7

STRIP AND TELL

After his escape from the up-tight Daley Auto Painting garage, Mark drove downtown toward the Algonquin. He still had to contact that Chinese merchant the professor told him about. He drove to the address. Inside, a tiny doll-like Chinese woman told Mark that Lee Wong was not feeling well today. Perhaps he would be in tomorrow.

Mark went on to the Algonquin and ate a big early lunch, then went up to his room and concentrated again on the newspaper clippings. He scanned the morning papers and clipped all follow-up stories. There wasn't much new. The *Times* had a roundup story on Black Gold, recounting the police records of two known members, and a summary of what little was known about the organization. It was frighteningly little, especially when he considered that the *Times* had been doing the digging. They had only two names, and both men were in prison. The *Times* did not mention the Daley Auto

Painting firm. At the end of the story they listed four other black action groups they considered in the violent category. Mark had not heard of any of them.

He sat down at the small desk and telephoned Professor Haskins in the Stronghold. Mark read the list of black action groups.

"Yes, Mark, one is familiar. I've seen a lot about the Black Mac. Why don't you check on it. It might give you some lead into Black Gold."

"Yes sir. I'll do it. You have anything else for me from your research?"

"Actually, no. I did discover there was a group known as Black Gold in Detroit for a while about six months ago. Then the leader was convicted on a heroin rap, and the bunch fell apart."

"You think they might be trying to spread out, build up units in other cities?"

"Sounds entirely possible."

Mark briefed Professor Haskins about the fanaticism he had found in his first encounter with the Daley operation.

"Move cautiously, Mark. I realize telling you that is like shouting into a hurricane. But Black Gold might go into hiding if they do get paid off by the city."

Mark agreed and said he'd call again when he could. He made some inquiries by phone and soon got the address of Black Mac. In the bathroom he looked at his black disguise and decided he wouldn't need it. He showered, scrubbing off the makeup, then dressed and slid Ava, the dart gun, into the spring clip-on holster at his belt which usually held the Colt Commander.

The dart gun was a tranquilizer weapon the professor had developed. When the tranquilizer fluid from a small needle-tipped dart entered the bloodstream, it immediately caused serious and painful muscle cramps, incapacitating the victim. Ten seconds after being hit, the man would be unconscious from the tranquilizer.

Mark found the headquarters of Black Mac just off Broadway on 116th Street. At first it looked like an old residence hotel. But as he came to the door he saw black power signs and emblems. A big poster on the door, in English and some foreign language, said: "Come in, Brother!"

Mark went in. The room was large, and looked like an old living room. Black power posters, advertising handbills and advertisements for black power books papered the walls. A big banner promoting a speaking engagement by Malcom X had been stretched from corner to corner. As soon as Mark opened the door a voice stabbed at him.

"What the hell you want, Whitey?"

Three tall, slender black youths in their twenties, wearing black berets and uniform-like tan pants and shirts, stood facing the door as if they had just taken up defensive positions.

"What the hell are you so belligerent about, Blackie?" Mark asked.

One of the youths swore and started forward in a classic head-down street-warfare charge. Mark waited. As the youth stormed toward him, the big Indian did not appear to move at all, but suddenly he was gone from where he had been, slipping to one side and smashing a wicked karate hand-chop to the back of the youth's neck. The black had time only to turn surprised eyes at Mark before he folded, crumpling forward in a somersault that left him flat on his back and unconscious.

The smaller of the other two blacks stared at him, then at his muscle man. He gulped.

"Look, man, like we ain't hunting no trouble, you dig? We just doing our own thing. What you want here?"

"Some information."

"Hell, we got lots of that." He sat down and waved his buddy away. The youth wore an Afro cut, and his eyes seemed large. He stared at Mark. "Information's our business, what kind you need?"

"Is that a uniform?"

"Sure."

"What is Black Mac?"

"That's us, man. Our black identity group. Ten of us. We push all kinds of black equal rights bits, speeches, lectures, books . . ."

"Plus extortion announcements and a subway explosion."

The black's eyes widened. "Oh, no, no sir! You can't hang that one on us. You the law? Some other cat did that."

Mark saw the third youth moving slowly, casually behind him. He would give him five more seconds.

"Mind if I take a look around?"

"Hell no, you can't look around. You got a warrant?"

Mark jumped to one side and saw a chair slash through the space he had vacated. It was attached to the third kid's hands. Before the chair hit the floor, Mark moved inside, drilled a hard right fist into the black's wide-open gut, and shot the other fist into his jaw. The boy dropped the chair and turned, one hand digging into his pocket. Mark kicked viciously, his boot toe hitting the underside of the arm just above the boy's wrist, snapping both bones. He followed with a hard hand-chop over the boy's heart, and the attacker slumped to the floor, blubbering with shock and pain, holding his shattered wrist.

Mark turned back to the Black Mac who still stood by the table.

"Son, I don't need a warrant. You have any objections?"

Slowly the boy's head shook. Fear showed in his eyes.

"Look around all you want. We got nothing to hide. We just don't like whites breaking in here and rousting us." The angry stare grew in fury. "We got every right to promote and push what we think is right for our people. We're publicity experts, and every minority's got a right to be heard, to have its say." He came around the table and bent over the boy with the broken wrist.

"You didn't have to kill him," the Black Mac leader said. "He's not a professional. I'm taking him to a hospital."

Mark checked a back door. It was locked.

"What's out there?"

"A hall. This is our only space. We rent it." He stood. "Look, I don't know who you are, but we're not militant. We're all college students, experts in promotion and public relations. We get news space and TV time. We make a lot of noise and attract attention, but we're nonviolent. None of our people has ever been arrested. Not for anything, man."

"I just saw two examples of your nonviolent work."

"They were all worked up. There was a killing not too long ago. Go ahead, look around."

Mark knew he would find nothing. The boys were zealots, dedicated, sincere, hard-working and square. His check of the room, files, drawers and closets produced nothing remotely connected with the bombing or extortion. He found records of news stories planted, a fair mimeograph machine, a small flyer called "The Black Truth," and eighty-five cents in the stamp box.

What the kid had said about minorities having a right to have their own say had stirred something inside Mark that David Red Eagle had first fanned into life when he had proved that Mark was half Cheyenne.

"You better get him to an emergency room," Mark said. He peeled two one-hundred-dollar bills from his money clip and handed them to the leader. "This should take care of the wrist. Remind the boy never to go for a knife again, or the next time he might be dead." The kid was still a sheep, not one of the goats.

Mark turned and walked out the front door and down to his car. He still drove the Continental. If he couldn't dig out anyone else connected with Black Gold, maybe they would spot the big car and come find him. He was making no secret of his intent.

Mark pulled Ava a little to one side as he slid into the car and drove slowly to the hotel. He'd stop by at his room and pick up some heavier armament, then do a stakeout on the painting garage.

It was a lead he knew would produce results. He took his time. It was only two o'clock, and he shouldn't be seen too long around the Daley place before dark. After closing time he was going to make a hard hit there and see what developed. He wouldn't need the black disguise.

The parking valet gobbled up the Continental and accepted the dollar insurance tip. Mark went upstairs. His room was on the seventh floor, and as he approached it, he tried to discern whether anyone had tampered with his door. He never could understand how those movie spies knew instantly when anyone had touched their hotel-room doors. Mark turned the key in the lock and went in.

He was trying to put together some kind of a timetable for Black Gold. Would they blow up something else? He wondered if they had collected their ransom. What would they hit next? Should he go in for a total smash tonight and dig out what they were hiding, or hold off?

"You sure don't spend much time in your room."

He snapped his head around toward the sound, his hand darting for his hip holster. But he didn't draw. The sight of an automatic pointed at him from behind the bathroom door stopped him. The voice was a woman's—and he'd heard it before.

She stepped around the door frame and he recognized her. Joanna Tabler, the lady cop who had been at the bar.

"Joanna, don't you ever knock? Or did you just earn your set of C.I.A. picklocks and decide to try them?"

She smiled and lowered the gun. "I really don't need this, because you and I are friends, right, Henry? And you *are* from California. I'm impressed." She dropped the gun into a large leather purse. She wore a white, long-sleeved blouse with ruffles down the front. The skirt was too short for the latest fashions, but just right to show off her perfect legs. Her hair seemed different, more formal, and he suspected she'd just come from having a shampoo and set.

"Henry, you really do have to help me. All I can say is that I'm a private investigator like yourself. And you know something about the Colonel that I don't."

Mark grinned. "And so you're ready to make any personal sacrifice, to throw yourself on my mercy..."

She shook her head, laughing softly. "Henry, I'm only desperate, not frantic." She smiled and walked toward him. "Henry, it could be a big score. I could take away one of the prime sources of explosives for groups like the Weathermen and this Black Gold thing. It's for the good of this town, and of the whole country."

Mark laughed. "Get a flag and wave it a little, it might help." He pulled the dart gun from his hip holster and pointed it at her.

"Henry, what in the world..."

"It's a tranquilizer gun, and it works." He motioned for her to sit on the edge of the bed.

"Joanna, I don't trust you. I'm alive because I *never trust anyone,* especially pretty girls who just happen to bump into me twice, and both times with a gun pointing at me. That tends to make you an unfriendly type. First I'll look in your bag."

She swung it over to him. Mark dumped it out on top of the dresser. It held over thirty items, including

©Lorillard 1973

Micronite filter.
Mild, smooth taste.
America's quality
cigarette.
Kent.

KENT

WITH
THE FAMOUS MICRONITE FILTER

DELUXE LENGTH

King Size or Deluxe 100's.

Kings: 16 mg. "tar," 1.0 mg. nicotine; 100's: 19 mg. "tar," 1.2 mg. nicotine;
Menthol: 18 mg. "tar," 1.3 mg. nicotine; av. per cigarette, FTC Report Sept. '73.

Try the crisp, clean taste
of Kent Menthol.

The only Menthol with the famous Micronite filter.

Warning: The Surgeon General Has Determined That Cigarette Smoking Is Dangerous to Your Health her .32 automatic, hair spray, combs, a compact and a small black book. On the front page had been written his Henry Joerden cover name and room number. Nothing else seemed out of place. He pushed the assortment back into her purse, then removed the magazine from the .32 and unchambered the remaining round. He put magazine and bullet in his pocket.

"Hey, that's mine," she said.

"I certainly hope so. Now for the important stuff. Strip, Joanna. Strip off every stitch, right down to mother nature."

She frowned. "My clothes? You're kidding! What good would that do?"

"Joanna, a man can learn a lot about a lady by what she hides in her brassiere."

"You mean it?"

"True."

Suddenly Joanna knew that he was serious. He was not going to rape her; he was looking for something. She didn't like the tone of his voice; maybe she had pushed him too far. That tone, and the look on his face, convinced her that he wasn't playing around. She began unbuttoning the fasteners down the front of the white blouse. She was a little frightened now, but not about undressing in front of a darkly handsome stranger. She was wondering just who he was. He was much more than a private operator, she knew that. He was on a case, but about what and for whom? Maybe the C.I.A.? She opened the last button and took off the blouse. For a moment she was surprised to notice how white her skin looked. She needed a week in the Florida sun, or in California.

He watched her, not with passion, but with that

91

cold, frightening dark gaze. There was a lethal feeling about him now that she hadn't sensed before. Was it because he felt himself threatened this time? She tossed the blouse to him and watched him examine it. He went over all the seams, bending and twisting them, looking for anything concealed. For a long moment he studied the buttons; he tried to pull one off, then to break it. When he couldn't he straightened the blouse and laid it carefully over a chair.

"More?" she asked.

His dark eyes came up again, and she wasn't sure if they were black now or dark brown. She shivered in spite of herself.

"Joanna, I'm interested in your clothes, not your body. You may not believe this, but I have seen girls naked before. Let's have your bra."

She reached back and unhooked it, realizing that the movement made her breasts thrust forward. Joanna let the bra slip down her arms, caught it and tossed it to him. She made no move to turn or to hide her breasts. He watched her large breasts sway and bounce with her movement, then began on the bra.

Between the cups he found a three-inch knife blade. It had no handle, only a blunt push-bar that fit neatly into the palm. At close range such a weapon was deadly. He held it up.

"Nice little toys the C.I.A. are handing out now. How long have you been with the agency?"

"I don't work for C.I.A."

He grunted and checked further. The small tracer bug was different from anything he had ever seen. It fit neatly into the underside of one cup, and was so flat that the slightly padded bra concealed it perfectly. He left it there.

"It must be reassuring to know that wherever you are, your control station knows exactly where your right breast is."

He was laughing at her, but she didn't care. If only he would help her get the evidence on the Colonel.

"The skirt, please."

She hesitated, then unzipped it and stepped out of it. He immediately found the two thin steel wires in the waistband. They were garroting wires. She had never used them. He pulled them out and put them beside the knife. He looked at her.

"My pantyhose? Now what could I hide . . ."

He held out one hand, motioning for her to give them to him. This was unreasonable. She felt anger rise as she began pulling down the hose. She sat on the bed and pulled the stocking parts off each leg, then threw the garment at him. That was when she saw she had the panties with the roses on them underneath the hose. At least she didn't have to look down.

He grabbed the hose and threw them back.

"Just stay where you are," he said. He stood beside her as she sat on the bed, and began checking her new hair set. Without damaging it, he picked out four small barrettes and held them out to her.

"What's in them? Just a simple knockout drug, or are they filled with some special C.I.A. poison?"

"If you know what they are, you should know what's in them. Who do you work with, our side or theirs?"

He snorted. "That will be the day." He kept all

93

of her weapons. "These gadgets make you more than a girl private eye. Who are you?"

"I'm someone who can help you, Henry. But would you either turn up the heat in here or let me get dressed?"

He stared at her. "You have a very fine body. Have you ever modeled? I bet you have. That's a model pose right now—beautiful, relaxed, striking. Very nice."

"Thanks. I did model for a while. Now may I please get dressed?"

"Yes."

She was a little disappointed as she reached for her pantyhose and slid into them. As she dressed, she began talking to him as she should have in the first place.

"Henry, let's call a truce. I'm not sure who you are, and you don't know who I am, but we can still help each other. I need some information I know damn well you have. I'll trade. Maybe I can help you in some way. Our firm has a tie-in with some of the biggest computer banks in the country. We can find out almost anything in five minutes." She finished putting on the pantyhose and realized she hadn't put on her bra yet. When she looked up she saw him watching her. She put her skirt on.

When she reached for her bra, her hand trembled. That was silly. She put her arms into her bra and reached behind to hook it. Why should she be nervous now?

"That computer of yours. Would it know anything about men with criminal records?"

She put on her blouse. "Of course. Complete. As a matter of fact, I ran you through. No record of ar-

94

rests. Then I checked your gun permit and it is legitimate, issued in San Bernardino, California."

"So?"

"So I know that Henry Joerden is a cover name. You see, this Henry Joerden has no Social Security number, no record of registering for the draft, no job, no military history, no fingerprints on file. For all practical purposes, Henry Joerden, you don't exist."

"It's my clean living." He stared at her, a slight frown on his dark face. He rubbed back the ends of his dark moustache, preening it as he often did when he was thinking. "Okay, lady spy, you've got a deal. If you can get what I want about one man, I'll play rat-fink for you on the Colonel and his buddies. But I can't give you the dope until I'm ready to leave town."

She fastened the last button on her blouse. "Can you be at my office tomorrow morning? I'll put your questions to the computers." She handed him a card from her purse.

"I'll be there. How about 9:00 a.m.?"

"Fine."

He had moved toward her to get the card. Now he bent forward and kissed her lips, softly. She felt a tremor in her body, and leaned toward him. His arms came around her and the soft kiss turned serious. Her arms went around his neck and she felt a stirring inside her.

When he pulled away she was grinning.

"I'm glad you waited to do that until I had my clothes back on," she said. She picked up her purse and went out the door.

Mark watched her leave. So many things she did —the way she tilted her head, the snap of her eyes,

95

her quick changes of expression—fascinated him. They were not the same mannerisms that Donna Morgan had used; yet there seemed to be something disturbingly familiar about them. He closed his eyes and sighed. He knew absolutely nothing about her. She was much more than she admitted, but he couldn't tell who she worked for. She could be on the other side—and he believed strongly that there still were two sides, in spite of the detente with Russia and the diplomatic hand-holding with Peking. She had to be working with a government agency of some kind.

If she wanted the Colonel, he would serve him up on a platter, but only after he checked to see if there was a real Mr. Daley behind the Daley Auto Painting outfit. He would watch her. He still didn't trust her completely. Joanna Tabler was much too beautiful and too smart for him to trust . . . at least for now.

8

SHOW-STOPPER BLAST

Mark checked his weapons, cleaning and oiling the pistols, then reloading them. He turned on the five o'clock news and sat in surprised silence as the TV newscaster recounted as much as anyone knew about the botched attempt to trap the Black Gold people at the payoff. They had found Lt. Larry Butler's personal car on the highway, totally burned, with the remains of the police officer inside. The two million dollars, the 1963 Chevrolet delivery car and the woman police lieutenant who drove it were all still unaccounted for.

"And so, ladies and gentlemen, the city of New York is two million dollars poorer tonight. That's your tax money right down the drain, and the police seem no closer to arresting or even finding the blackmailers than they were before this Black Gold band disrupted our island with threats and acts of violence two nights ago. Whoever Black Gold is, they must be laughing at the inept and downright bungling city

97

administration and police force tonight. A few terrorists have made a laughingstock of our fair city. Oh, yes, it was the mayor's suggestion that the money be paid, so the police could try to nab the persons making the pickup."

Mark switched it off. So now they had the money, the two million in untraceable twenty-dollar bills. What would they do? Lay low and spend some money? No, it didn't seem reasonable. The best defense is always a good offense. If Mark were in the Black Gold camp he'd vote for another attack, another hit while the police were still trying to get their bearings.

Mark put off his hard hit on the Daley Auto Painting firm. He wanted to check out the computer report tomorrow with Joanna. It might turn up something new he could use against Daley. And in some way it might tie the man in solidly with Black Gold.

He telephoned Lee Wong's store, and recognized the small woman's voice when she answered.

"Mrs. Wong, I'm a good friend of Professor Willard Haskins who taught at Columbia."

"Oh, yes, we very good friends Professor Haskins too."

"I'm in town from California on a project for him, and he said I should call Mr. Wong and talk to him about a very important matter. How could I reach him?"

A moment later he had another telephone number, which he dialed. The voice that answered came across the line softly, with a strange, polite caution.

"Yes?"

"Mr. Wong, I'm a friend of Professor Willard Haskins, who used to teach at Columbia."

"Oh, yes, I know the professor well."

"He said I should call you, perhaps talk with you. Would that be possible?"

There was a long pause. "Could you describe the professor for me? I must be careful."

Mark did as he was asked, adding that the professor had shaved off the beard because it was too much bother.

A long sigh came across the line. "Yes, I believe you do know the professor. Where does he live?"

Mark told him precisely, explaining the workings of the Stronghold camouflage.

"Yes, you have been there. I am cautious because some persons wish to harm me."

"Chinese?"

"Yes."

"Would that include Soo Lin?"

A quick intake of breath whistled in the earpiece. "EYIIIIIIIIIIIIIII! You know this evil one?"

"She tried to shoot me this morning, but missed."

"Then you do not work with her?"

"No. The professor and I are trying to find out what we can about an Afro-Chinese alliance. I talked to John Washington yesterday."

"Mr. Washington is a good man." Wong paused, and Mark wished he could see the Chinese's face, to judge and weigh what he was saying.

"I think Soo Lin is working with Black Gold in this extortion racket," Mark said. "Can you tell me anything that might help me to stop them?"

"Ah. . . . you sound like great gong in temple, yet even in the hidden places your words ring with a sage's wisdom."

"When can we have a talk?"

"Tonight my car will call for you."

"I'll be in front of the Algonquin hotel."

"The car will be there precisely at 6:30," Mr. Wong said. "I will not be in it. There will be a folded piece of white paper under the passenger's-side windshield-wiper. It is a blue Mercedes."

Mark said goodbye and hung up. He had no idea if the meeting would help, but he couldn't overlook any leads.

He emptied his suitcase and made a quick trip to the parking garage, where he selected certain equipment, arms and supplies from the Continental's trunk. He needed a more versatile selection in his room for quick use. As he went back into the hotel he realized that in his suitcase were enough illegal arms and explosive devices to put him in a federal prison for thirty years. Upstairs he looked over every item, then locked the suitcase and put it in the closet, arranging it so that he would know if it had been disturbed.

At 6:25 he stood in front of the Algonquin, waiting for his meeting with Mr. Chang. The car came precisely on time, and the driver jumped out and opened the rear door for Mark. Neither spoke, but Mark was aware that he was examined critically. He was sure the Chinese driver noticed the slight bulge of the holster on his right hip under his coat. They drove for a dozen blocks, then stopped beside a dark doorway. A man left the shadows and quickly got into the car. Mark saw he was Chinese.

"So, Professor Haskins' friend. It is good to meet you. Don't bother with a name. I'm sure it wouldn't be your real one anyway."

Mark watched the small man through the dim and changing light patterns. He seemed to be about sixty, with gray hair, glasses and several gold-capped front teeth.

"First let me answer the question you must have about my seclusion, my secrecy. Certain Chinese individuals have sworn to kill me. It is because I would not cooperate with them in convincing the Chinese community here in Manhattan to help them finance some adventure. Now I realize that this adventure is the alliance with Black Gold and the extortion plan."

"Then the local Chinese have no part in it?"

"Not at all. Certain elements in the old families have joined with the blacks. Soo Lin is a vile creature who came here from China to coerce us into helping. We have dual Chinese and U.S. citizenship. China insists on this no matter how much we deny it, or how long we have lived in this country. Many of us have been here for generations, but we still have relatives in China—so they have a powerful weapon."

"But you talked against this cooperation."

"True—then I went into hiding. I told all Chinese to deny this foreign devil, to send her packing. I insisted they must defy this insignificant girl child with the red banner and the bloody hand. Already she has killed two men here, both my good friends."

"Sir, do you know where she operates? Any headquarters?"

He shook his head. "I wish I did. I cannot help you on that. The girl is straight from Red China. She is their representative here. She must be a high-ranking agent in the Chinese secret service apparatus."

"Mr. Wong, have you heard her use any names, mention any places here in Manhattan?"

"No. She is very cautious."

101

"Do you know a man named Daley, or the Daley Auto Painting Company in Harlem?"

"No. This is all I can say. I have told you everything that seems to apply. I will return to seclusion now."

Mark looked out the car window and saw that they had come to a stop in front of the Algonquin. The doorman reached for the handle.

"I thank you, sir," Mark said, and left the car. He didn't use that term of respect to many men, but this small Chinese was one who deserved it. Mark watched the Mercedes pull away and vanish around the corner.

It was a little after eight when Mark went into the hotel dining room. He ordered every side dish of vegetables on the menu, a seafood cocktail and a huge chef's salad. Red Eagle would not have been proud of his choices.

At six the next morning Mark was up. He put in a tough twenty minutes exercising, finishing with a run around the block three times. He almost got arrested twice. He had just finished showering and was listening to the morning news when a dramatic announcement came. It was another recorded flash from Big Daddy Squirley. The newscaster moved into it smoothly.

"Ladies and gentlemen, the following recorded message has just been sent to us by Big Daddy Squirley, an all-night radio personality on our affiliate AM radio station. He orginally broke the story about Black Gold and the bombing of the 72nd Street subway station. This latest threat could have equally serious consequences for the citizens of New York.

Here is a tape recording of a telephone call by a spokesman for Black Gold."

The newscaster gave a signal, and adapted a listening posture as the recorded voice came through.

"Listen, Whitey, you out there in Manhattan and the Bronx and Brooklyn. We've got a message for you, baby. It's like this. The cops let you down, gave away two million dollars to us Black Gold cats. Yeah, that's just a start, man. You think not having subways is rough? Wait, man, wait till I lay the next one on you. Our target now is all them damn radio and television broadcasting antennas. The ones for radio, TV and the police radio. Oh, we know where they are, baby, *all the muthas*, and we're not working on just one. No way, man. We gonna blow up every mutha sons of bucks of them. No TV, no radio, no pig cop calls. Now won't that be a gas! We gonna shoot the works mighty soon, unless we get the word that our good mayor and the city bigshots gonna cough up a cool three million bucks.

"That's right, baby, three million, in three suitcases, in used twenties, just like before. And we want the cash delivered by a midget in one of them little Honda cars. Don't worry, Commish, baby, our deal is still on for your percentage. Nice work on that first pass. We like doing business with you, partner. Just don't let on to the damn mayor. Be at your phone like at three this afternoon for the word how and when."

The newscaster took over again, sounding properly grave.

"And that, viewers, is the latest in what is becoming a series of demands and extortions by the Black Gold militant organization. The group is thought to be headquartered somewhere here in Manhattan. Police have come up with an absolute zero in their efforts to track down these men called blackmailers by some, and hijackers by others who are literally stealing the Borough of Manhattan right out from under us."

Mark turned off the set. The broadcasting antennas—blacking out TV, radio and police. It would be a massive, crippling stroke. Most of the antennas were high on top of skyscrapers like the Empire State Building. That could mean some explosions at high altitudes, with fallout on the streets below. A lot of people could get killed that way.

Mark made a quick check of the *Times*, but found no report of a death by shooting in a Harlem garage. The Daley Auto Painting firm looked better by the minute. He finished dressing, shaved, trimmed his moustache with his little scissors, and decided he was ready.

He was fifteen minutes early when he arrived at Joanna Tabler's office, but already the wheels of industry were whirling. The name on the sixtieth floor read: Diogenes Investigations Inc. Mark had dressed for the occasion, expecting the office to be as plush as the address. He had on a brown pin-stripe shirt, brown tie and a deep gray corduroy sports coat. The girl at a reception desk smiled when he asked to see Miss Tabler, and asked if he had an appointment.

Two minutes later, another bright, pants-clad young girl ushered him into an inner office with Joanna's name on the door. It was a corner setup, with a thick carpet, good original oil paintings on the walls, and a free-form desk of polished cherrywood that had nothing on it except one file folder.

104

Joanna stood and smiled. She wore a sleek, form-fitting knit dress of pale blue that was a marvel of body advertising.

"Good morning—let's see, your name is Henry this time, isn't it? Or did you change it since yesterday? Are you going to make me strip again?"

Mark laughed and shook his head. She had done something with her hair that gave it an entirely different look, like a silver-blonde waterfall.

"Right now I'd rather look at your computers than your etchings. Are you awake this early?"

"It's the middle of the day for me—and the computers. They put in a twenty-four-hour work day." She hesitated, her eyes staring hard at his. "You know I want that warehouse. After I help you, you're going to give me the address. Right?"

"Right, but not today."

"When?"

"Soon—two, three days."

She scowled, then shrugged. "Three days at the outside. Now, what's our victim's name?"

She scribbled on a paper as he talked.

"Daley. He has a business on 132nd Street called Daley Auto Painting. I don't know his first name."

She took a telephone from one of her desk drawers and made a call, then another. Just as she hung up, the phone sounded a soft chime and she answered it. She listened a moment, made a note and looked up.

"Your man's first name is Abdul, which must make him a Black Muslim. The name is in the machines now and we'll be getting a printout from our local source very soon."

"Just like that?"

"Diogenes Investigations is not limited to the pedestrian."

Mark shook his head. "Is that your standard opening with a new client? A client who isn't a part of the U.S. government?"

"This is a private firm. We pay our way with complete and efficient investigations about anything, from a runaway heiress to tracking down a stock issue."

"How does it show on the books? I mean do you actually bill the C.I.A. for services rendered?"

"Damn you . . ." She took a deep breath and stood up. Joanna had promised herself a dozen times that she would not let him make her angry this time. He was so impudent, so nagging, so . . . She sighed and punched the telephone button.

"Bring in what you have so far," she ordered.

A moment later a door opened at the side of the room and a thin, quiet-looking girl came in with two lengths of computer readout paper, each about a foot long. She gave them to Joanna and left without a word.

Joanna skimmed the first one quickly, smiled and passed it on to Mark. He read it slowly.

DALEY, ABDUL, AKA DALEY, JAMES. 25 YEARS. NEGRO. SIXTY INCHES TALL. 109 POUNDS. BORN IN HARLEM 1949 TO MILDRED J. DALEY. FATHER UNKNOWN. ABANDONED AGE SIX. IN VARIOUS FOSTER HOMES. RUNAWAY 8 TIMES. JUVENILE RECORD EXTENSIVE. TRIED AS ADULT 1966 ON MURDER CHARGE IN BLACK PANTHER SHOOTOUT. HUNG JURY TWICE. SUBJECT FREED.

Mark looked up. "There's going to be more?"

"This is just a start, from the local computer bank. We'll also check military records, the F.B.I., Social Security . . ."

Mark couldn't keep from staring at her. He watched the way she moved, the small motions of her hands, the slant of her head, her long graceful neck.

"Miss Tabler, I do think I've underestimated you."

Her hazel eyes shifted from the printout to his face. She didn't know what to say. It was one of the few faintly complimentary things he had said to her. She looked back at the paper in her hands without seeing it.

"You have an interesting friend here."

"He's no friend. I've never met him. But I hope to soon."

She handed him the other paper, and he scanned it. On it was a juvenile record, of the sort which usually is confidential. Daley had a history of arrests, both as a juvenile and an adult, up to about four years ago. But his record was absolutely clean since that time.

"The warehouse address, Henry."

"Later. They took me there blindfolded. I didn't even see which direction we went in, and couldn't tell how far away it was. When we got inside the building we went down some iron stairs to a basement, and there it was. Anything you want for a small war. Grenades, rifles machine guns, rocket launchers, explosives . . ."

"I thought you knew the address."

"Later." Mark kept reading, and when the thin girl came in with more papers he took half and speed-read them. He nodded when he checked the military

107

experience. Abdul Daley was an expert with all small arms, and a qualified explosives expert. Still, there was one element missing.

"You find anything about drug involvement, hard stuff?"

She lifted her brows. "No, there was nothing in the printouts I covered. He's clean with narco here."

"It doesn't fit his pattern. He can't support his operation on that car painting business."

"What operation?"

Mark wiped one big hand over his face. "He sells soft ice-cream bars to diabetics."

She laughed.

He knew he had to be on to something. A guy with Daley's record and background, his less-than-honorable army discharge—and Soo Lin in the same complex. It just didn't add up to anything but fishy. He thought about it. Soo Lin could have a connection with the Chinese supply of poppy, opium and heroin. He would give Mr. Wong another call. The quiet Oriental must know a great deal that he hadn't volunteered.

Mark began folding the printouts and stood. "Can I take these with me?"

"If your memory improves about that warehouse."

"It will, in three days. The Colonel has a few friends here who would be upset with me if I told you now."

She left the safety of the big desk and walked to the window. Mark liked the way her sleek body moved under the knit material. He could tell she wore no bra today.

At the floor-to-ceiling window she turned and

watched him. "This client of yours, is he interested in Mr. Abdul Daley?"

"Of course; that's why I'm here."

"Your client has strange interests."

"Luck of the draw."

"You will remember that warehouse address?"

He put down the papers and walked toward her. His quick surge of emotion surprised him. He beat it down and put his hands on her shoulders, pulling her gently forward. His kiss was hard; his arms went around her, pulling her tightly against his chest.

When he let her go and leaned back, her eyes were still closed. She opened them lazily, her arms around him.

"Yes, I do like your moustache. It kisses good."

"I know that's going to help my memory." He looked at her. "You ever go out for dinner?"

She nodded, a soft, cautious smile lighting her beautiful face.

"I'll call. Got to check out a few people."

"Please do call."

He walked away from her and turned. "That dress is a hell of a lot better than red pants." He picked up the papers and left the room.

Downstairs he slid into a phone booth. It took him only a moment to remember the number Mrs. Wong had given him the previous night.

Someone came on the phone at the first ring.

"Mr. Wong, I'm the professor's friend. I have some questions."

"Yes, I thought you might."

"Did Soo Lin hint in any way that there might be drugs involved?"

"At our first meeting she told me there was a tre-

109

mendous market here for her special 'refined sugar' as she called it. She said I could get in on it, since her current dealer was becoming troublesome. I threw her out."

"Then she made the threats?"

"Later. Too many of our people are involved in narcotics. Many think just because they are Chinese ... One particularly vicious operation uses twelve to fourteen-year-old Chinese girls as pushers. I've tried to stop it without hurting the girls involved, but can't find a way. This one is run by a man I know only as Abdul."

"I mentioned an Abdul Daley last night. Could he be the one?"

"I do not know."

"Is your man black? And about five feet tall?"

"Yes. I've heard them talk about him. He's small and black. No Chinese would involve children with narcotics."

Mark scowled at the phone. It was one of the tricks pushers were using to get around the tough new New York State narcotics laws. The maximum penalty for the sale of one ounce or more of hard stuff, or illegal possession of two ounces, was life in prison. That included a mandatory jail term of fifteen to twenty-five years before parole eligibility. The new law made the penalty for drug pushing the same as for murder in New York. No wonder the pushers were using kids to hold the junk and complete the sales on the street. Anyone under sixteen was immune from the tough law.

Two minutes later Mark had an address. He wasn't sure if it was still good, because the drop and bank

110

changed locations every two months, but Mr. Wong said it might be good.

Mark brushed the Colt Commander .45 on his right hip, under his jacket. It rested securely in its spring-clip holster made of soft deerhide.

He left the phone booth and hurried to his car. He felt a sense of urgency. It was beginning to tie together. Abdul Daley must be the honcho behind the girl pushers. That would bankroll him for more ambitious projects.

Mark found the address at the edge of the Chinese community. It was a Chinese grocery and health-food store. He checked his .45. It was loaded and locked, with one round in the chamber and seven more in the magazine.

He closed the Continental's door and walked into the small grocery, fingering a blue flint arrowhead in his pocket. The glint in his eyes spelled death.

9

BLUE FLINT DEATH

When Mark stepped into the cramped, cluttered store there was only one person there, a small Chinese man with long hair and pimples. He looked about twenty.

Inscrutable he was not. His tongue flicked over dry lips. He tried not to look at a small opening leading into the rear, but his eyes kept drifting that way. When Mark walked up to him the youth didn't know what to do with his hands. He was covering up something and was nervous about it.

"Help you?" his high voice squeaked.

"Yeah, but I'm selling," Mark said, stepping straight at him. The boy had no opportunity to dodge. Mark pointed his finger at the youth, then at the window. The Chinese looked where Mark pointed, and as he did, Mark powered a short karate chop against the bridge of his nose. The hand moved only a foot, but the Oriental gurgled and began to sag. Mark caught him, draping him over a stool behind the counter.

The blow wasn't meant to kill, but to create a massive shock wave to the skull and especially the optic nerve, which would be useless for half an hour, after which the victim would develop double vision for up to twenty-four hours.

Mark moved silently toward the back room. Hearing muted voices from the rear of the store, he flipped back his jacket and drew the .45 Commander. When he stepped through the opening he found himself in a storage area. Opposite him stood a closed wooden door. Mark went to it and listened. The voices were louder. He tried the knob silently. Locked.

Mark took one step back, then kicked forward with the flat of his right foot, putting all his 185 pounds into the blow. The cheap catch-lock snapped and the door slammed open.

Mark jumped into the room at the same instant. Two black men were hunched over a table, carefully measuring a white powder into plastic packets, weighing each packet on a delicate chemist's scale. There was a hot iron ready to seal each packet of white heroin.

The two men looked up at the .45 muzzle and froze. One man's hand had been in his lap under the table. Mark saw the shoulder muscles tighten as the hand moved.

At that moment Mark wished he had his silencer. Swiftly he flipped the .45 to his left hand and flexed his right wrist, releasing the knife he had strapped there. The four-inch blade slid forward, point first, as he jerked his arm sharply backwards. In a split second he was gripping the handle of the knife in his right hand.

He threw the small weapon with the swiftness and accuracy of a bullet. The steel drove deeply into the black man's chest. His hand had just closed around a .38 in his pocket. The man stared down at the blade as it slammed into him, surprise washing over his face, then alarm. Finally a sudden desperation clouded his features, and he slumped in the chair, dead.

Mark motioned for the other man to stand.

"Lace your hands on top of your head and turn around," Mark barked at him. The black turned, shivering so hard he could hardly lock his hands.

"Jeez, man. Take it easy. You just killed Willy."

"You're next if you so much as breathe hard, understand?" Mark pushed the man against the wall and spread his legs and hands wide. He frisked the man quickly, taking a .38 from his belt and a switchblade from his right leg. Mark stashed the hardware on the far end of the table, then took a small blue-tipped syringe from the flap on his boot. He broke off the protective tip covering the needle end and showed the shooter to the creep against the wall.

"Badass, you ever seen a dog with rabies, a mad dog?"

The man's eyes rolled. Sweat beaded his forehead. He nodded.

"That's what you're gonna have in about twenty seconds. See this needle? It's filled with live rabies germs. Guy down in Mexico makes them up for me. I slam this into your arm, you'll go into the most painful kind of death anybody ever thought up. You want that?"

114

"God no. Christ, what is this, a heist? Take the goddamn money, take the junk. It's all yours, man!"

"Who's running this drop?" Mark barked.

The black man's eyes darted toward the door. "You know I can't tell you that."

Mark moved toward him with the needle in one hand, the .45 in the other.

"Who's the top dog, your supplier?"

"Damnit, you know . . ." He looked at the needle and sweat came down past his eyes in small glistening rivers. "Promise you won't stab me with that thing if I tell?"

"Sure, man. What I got against you?"

"You damn sure? I seen a dog die like that once." He sighed, looked at Mark. "He's some black cat. I only met him once. I work through another guy. This cat's name is Abdul. Only name I know, I swear."

"He's a little guy, about five feet tall?"

"Yeah, little and bitch mean."

Mark lunged forward, ramming the needle into the black man's upper arm, pushing the plunger with his thumb, shooting the two cubic centimeters of juice into the black flesh.

When Mark leaned back, he left the needle dangling in the arm.

"Present for you, you dirty sonofabitch."

"Goddamnit, you promised me!"

"So sue me. Sit down in the corner and it won't take so long to take effect. Where's the cash?"

The man slumped to the floor. His head came up and he tried to scream, but already the fluid was doing its work. Mark always worried that the sodium pentathol wasn't going to do the job. The black would be unconscious for twenty minutes.

115

Mark took the rest of the kilo of heroin and dumped it in a small sink at one side of the room. He washed it down the drain, leaving only two papers of the joy juice on the table. It was enough for evidence, but not enough for some crooked cop to hide so he could sell it later.

He found the bank, all the cash neatly bundled in a small black doctor's satchel. It was in fives, tens and twenties. He had no idea how much money was there. Mark bent over the dead man, pulled his blade free and wiped off the blood on the man's fancy jacket. Then he slid the knife back into its leather home on his right wrist and snapped it in place.

Mark took one of the flint arrowheads and jammed the point hard into the dead man's chest wound. It stuck. This would be the first time the press heard about the arrowheads; now they would know that the Penetrator was in the big city. It might help him flush out the Black Gold gang.

Five minutes later, the Penetrator left the store and used a phone booth two blocks down the street. He watched from the Continental as two unmarked cars snarled up to the Chinese grocery store. An ambulance came, and then two prowl cars with blinking lights. The uniformed men brought out the tall Negro, who was still groggy but could walk. Mark laughed. They had an iron-clad heroin case all wrapped up for the D.A.

Mark wasted no time now. He wanted to hit Abdul before the news of this bust got to him. He drove to a deserted street and checked the Continental's trunk. In one locked suitcase he found what he wanted—another loaded .45 clip for his pocket, and a fragmentation grenade. It was not the latest kind of grenade, but one of the old pineapple type. And it was fresh. He'd had Sal Mitzuzaki tear down a dozen two weeks before, and put in new primer and powder. He knew this one would go off when he wanted it to. He locked the trunk and drove north into Harlem.

The Penetrator had decided he wouldn't use a disguise this time. It was to be a hard, fast hit in daylight. He had to know what they were protecting in that warehouse. He wondered if it now included the two million dollars in payoff money.

Mark parked half a block from Daley Painting. He had his .45 and the frag grenade in his pocket. He walked quickly up the sidewalk to the front door. Inside, the office seemed deserted. He ran to the backshop door and opened it. One man pounded methodically on a battered car's fender. Three more black men stood nearby. When they saw the Penetrator they moved toward him.

"Outside, you sonofabitch. We don't want whatever you selling," one of them shouted.

Mark didn't move. The three walked closer. All of them were large and looked angry.

"What the hell, man? We told you to split," another one said. "Now you get your ass out of here before we pitch it out."

Mark looked at him, scowling. "What's your name?"

They rushed him.

The Penetrator had the .45 out before they had covered half the distance. They halted and began to back up.

"Down on the floor, on your faces, all of you," the Penetrator snapped.

117

They broke and ran in three directions. Mark saw one man grabbing at his belt for a weapon. He instinctively fired at the upper torso, the kill zone, and saw his .45 round tear into the man's side, moving toward his heart. The man stumbled and fell, rolling into a pile of junked fenders. He lay still.

Before the Penetrator could duck behind a pillar, a shot whizzed past his head. He whirled, and saw a new entrant in the duel at the head of an exposed stairway twenty yards across the open two-storied garage. Mark angled a quick shot his way, then threw himself behind an old car.

One of the blacks had the same idea; as Mark reached the car he noticed the man's feet on the other side. Mark waited for him to move around the end of the rig, then blasted one .45 slug through his forehead, ending a short, tough life. The impact spun the man backwards, his pistol sliding from dead fingers and clattering to the cement.

The black man who had been working on the car threw down his tools and sprinted out the big roll-up door. Mark let him go; he was a sheep, not one of the hard-core criminals.

He worked his way around another car, heard movement behind him and waited. A man sprinted for the steps. Mark held his weapon at arm's length, gripped his right hand with his left and fired twice. The second slug stopped the runner. The man twisted and fell, spinning into an open gallon can of paint, jolting it into the air and splattering it over himself and the floor of the garage. It was a bright red. He sat up and fired a small-caliber weapon at Mark. The next .45 slug ripped into the black chest and slammed him backwards into more paint cans.

As soon as he fired the last shot, the Penetrator turned, a wild instinct causing his senses to tighten. Someone was behind him!

He saw the gun poking out from a pile of boxes twenty feet away. As it lined up on him, Mark dove to one side, rolled over and heard the sound of the air parting as a slug sliced past his face. He returned the fire with a pair of closely spaced shots through the cardboard containers, just to the right of where the gun had been.

When the booming roar of the .45 quieted, Mark could hear nothing at all. Not a footstep, not a whimper. He waited. One man still held the high ground on the stairs, and one could be behind the boxes. He darted from cover to cover as he retreated toward the pile of boxes, keeping himself out of sight of the stairs. As he made his last rush across an open space he heard a shot kick up cement chips at his feet, but he was safe behind another wrecked car.

He checked the boxes and saw the remains of the third of the trio of hard cases. Both slugs had entered the man's mouth, tearing away much of his lower jaw, slamming on into his throat and chest, turning him into a dead mass of bloody meat.

The Penetrator realized he had spent too much time here. Police must already be on the way. He dropped a blue flint arrowhead on the dead man's chest and stormed the stairway. There was no fire against him. He checked the rooms upstairs but found no one, and nothing incriminating. No C-4, no weapons, no clue that Black Gold was ever here.

Mark ran back to the ground floor auto shop, jammed another arrowhead into one of the dead men, and faded away through a side door.

He had settled down in his Continental half a block away and started the engine when the first squad car careened around the corner from the other end of the block, siren wailing, red light flashing. As Mark drove away he passed three more police cars, but none of the cops even looked his way.

Lt. Art Chuchulski swore when he looked at the carnage in the painting shop. Three dead men, all black. No witnesses, no suspects, evidently no survivors. The cash register inside the office had not been touched. What the hell was this?

He pushed back a reporter who was looking at one of the bodies. "Get the hell outahere!" Lt. Chuchulski roared.

"Come on Lieutenant, give us the story. That's a real arrowhead in that guy's body, blue flint. I've seen them before. We had a story an hour ago about another body with a blue flint arrowhead in his chest. Is this the work of that Penetrator guy, the crime buster from Los Angeles and Washington? He goes around killing off the bad guys."

"What? What the hell you talking about? You nuts? Get out of here and let me do my job. I got three killings and no witnesses."

"But it could be the Penetrator, right?"

"Sure, could have been you." Lt. Chuchulski moved to his right. "Hey, get that damn camera out of here. No pictures until the medics get through!"

He pushed the photographer back. "Goddamnit, you guys ain't gonna make no circus outa my precinct. Just clear out, all you news nuts, TV too, out, out!" Lt. Chuchulski watched the uniformed men move the reporters back to the big doors. The corpse doctors would be here soon, then they could get all the blood out of sight. What a slaughter. But what the hell was this arrowhead jazz? He'd gone over that flyer on Lt. Butler's desk, the one about the Penetrator. That fruitcake wouldn't dare mess around in New York. Still, those damn arrowheads . . .

He knew the press would have a field day with this one. He just hoped to Christ that the punks on the meat blocks here had long records, tough ones, that would help. But arrowheads? Jesus H. Kreist! What kind of a damn zoo was this precinct turning into?

10

THE FIRE-KNIFE PLAY

Only a few visitors had braved the chill late January weather for a look at the city from the observation floor of the Empire State Building. Only one elevator was operating, and the employees went through the motions, watching the clocks, wishing the time would speed by faster.

A hundred and five floors below, in one of the subbasements of the tall structure, a guard sat at his post. The maintenance crews were arriving. Two young blacks came through in their coverall uniforms, flashed badges lazily at the guards and moved inside. A short time later two more young Negroes walked through, waving a hello with their badges as they talked together. The guards saw nothing unusual about the four. Dozens of men and women had passed through their gate for that shift. But the four blacks separated and moved leisurely to pre-selected locations.

Jinx Marshall curled into a small ball in back of

some air-conditioning ductwork on sub-level four. The spot was in a little-used hallway and he was safe from anything except an all-out search. There would probably be no one in the area all night.

Bo Atler spent some time cleaning the mirrors in the male employees' rest room on sub-level three. It was the first time he'd spent much time in such a fancy bathroom. He stared at everything, very impressed. Once another maintenance man came in, but Bo was hard at work on a mirror. The other man relieved himself, waved and left. After an hour, Bo got tired; he retreated to one of the toilet booths and closed the door. He could wait there just as well, sitting down.

Wonder Roberts had the least exposed position. He picked the lock on a door on sub-level six marked: "Danger: High Voltage. No Admittance." Inside he found it exactly as Abdul said it would be—only a little more cramped. The room was just under ten feet square, and warm. It was loaded with electrical components, what looked like a transformer or junction box and lots of wires and metal boxes of all sizes. He checked off a dozen items he needed to find against a list he took from his pocket. Then Wonder Roberts grinned and settled down against the wall.

This one would be a piece of cake. For a moment he frowned at the big box beside him, then he patted the plastic explosive that was wrapped around his waist under his uniform and laughed. None of these boxes was gonna hurt him; just the opposite. He closed his eyes and went to sleep.

Abdul Daley felt uncomfortable in his janitor's uniform. They had researched the place carefully and this was the only way they could get in to do the job right. He shifted the burden of the C-4 explosive wrapped around his stomach and snorted. Honkey was gonna catch it again! He had worked here for two months six years ago, and now was glad to see that most of the procedures were just the same. He rode a service elevator to the top floor, then went to the sub-levels, nodding at guards, chattering with workers. Abdul carried a clipboard, as his supervisor used to. When men saw the board they automatically got busy.

He suddenly felt like going into every men's room and writing on the mirrors: "Black Gold was here!" A moment later he knew the idea was childish. Instead he went over the plans again. The maintenance crew was supposed to get off work at 1:00 a.m. He hoped they hadn't changed that. After the janitors left, the real work would begin.

Three hours later, Abdul watched through a slit in a nearly closed door as the last of the maintenance people checked out and the guard on duty inside the big door marked off the log. At last the guard closed the post, moving out the doors and down a long hall.

The moment the door banged shut, Abdul ran down the hall to the steps and on down to the sixth sub-level. He could not risk the use of a service elevator with its tell-tale floor indicator. He ran down the steps, anxious now to get at the job. Jinx and Bo were both there, waiting for him. They gave him a thumbs-up sign and he knocked on the door marked "Danger."

Roberts opened the door and waved. He pointed to the high-energy cables and the sheathed coaxial and heavy lines near them.

"Damn, must be half the radio and TV stations in town that broadcast outa here. You know that shaped charge idea? Use shaped ones to blow just the police and TV stuff? No deal. Negative. Just won't work, man."

"So, what's the alternative?" Abdul asked.

"We blow up the whole damn works. The high-voltage and broadcast cables'll get all messed up together and nobody'll be able to touch nothing until somebody kills the juice. I'd say at least two days before they make sense out of it and get back on the air."

"Cops got an auxiliary tower, case this one gets zapped?" Bo asked.

"Who the hell cares?" Abdul said. "They'll get the damn message. Stuff the putty on and let's get with it. We ain't trying to knock out every station in town. I got the word the police land cable comes through here and goes to a repeater antenna up there on top the building somewhere. I ain't about to climb out on top a mile in the sky and fix any charges. We do it here and take what we can get. Some dude told me the networks use the antenna up there too, but they send the signal to the tower by microwave. So we don't get them, tough, we get the ones we want, the honkey pig's radio."

All four of them peeled the plastic strips of C-4 explosive off their bodies and laid them out for Roberts. It took Wonder and Abdul only ten minutes to work the plastic C-4 into the shapes they wanted and to press it in place around cables, along conduits, next to heavy boxes, and on every piece of exposed cable they could find.

125

They set seven timed electrical fuses to blow in fifteen minutes.

When Abdul had clicked the last fuse dial, they closed the door, made sure they all still wore their soft white gloves, then took the stairs up to the first sub-level. They got out of the sub-floors into a by-pass corridor by picking a lock, then walked past the main door guards, grumbling about damn mandatory overtime.

Outside, a cruising car picked them up on the corner. Inside the car a special police band radio stuttered and chattered with police codes and call letters. Abdul looked at his watch.

"Almost four minutes left before it blows," he said.

Somebody turned the car's radio on to a music station. The seconds ticked by as the car headed north toward Harlem. No one said a word. Abdul's face was set; he feared the worst, while hoping for total victory.

The watches came up again.

"Twenty seconds by my watch," Abdul said.

Each of them counted down the time. The twenty seconds stuttered past. Abdul's face twisted in fury.

Then the police radio went dead; only a faint humming came over the frequency.

"Right on!" Abdul shouted, and the others in the car cheered. They began checking the commercial radio stations, and found three of them not broadcasting.

The car went north on the West Side Highway, past the George Washington Bridge to Inwood Hill Park, where it stopped. One by one the men stripped off their Empire State Building maintenance-man coveralls and threw them into the parked car. The

126

last man out tossed a book of flaming matches into the car, where two gallons of gasoline had been dumped. The car was a raging fire in seconds.

Twenty minutes later they were safe in their new headquarters building, still congratulating each other. Abdul drank a toast to the Black Gold warriors, then caught Soo Lin's hand and led her away.

Mark, along with most New Yorkers, first heard of the knocking off the air of half the city's radio and TV stations, as well as the police radio relays, the next morning. Big Daddy Squirley had another message from Black Gold. It reminded the city fathers to pay up that day, as instructed, or the rest of the radio and TV antennas would be blasted. "Commish, Baby, you remember the time and place, and don't forget the midget. He won't even have to lift all that money."

Mark looked at the morning papers. One had an eight-column banner headline: PENETRATOR RAVAGES HEROIN PUSHERS. Another emphasized the rumor that some kill-crazy ex-war veteran had shot up all of Manhattan. One paper tried to link the killing splurge with Black Gold. Police had little to say on the matter. Two papers ran full accounts of the Penetrator's supposed exploits in Los Angeles, Las Vegas and Washington, D.C. Each paper said there was no information about the Penetrator's real identity, or about whether he only killed dope pushers and hoodlums. The tone of the stories was favorable, making the Penetrator a kind of combination of Robin Hood and Batman, out to rid the town of a lot of undesirable characters.

Mark looked at the stories and nodded. They

could be a big help to him, if he used the publicity correctly.

He picked up a long envelope which he had found stuffed under his door when he had brought in the papers He deliberately had left it for last. Only two people in town knew where he stayed: Joanna Tabler and Lee Wong. He opened the sealed envelope and took out a sheet of paper bearing the dignified letterhead of Diogenes Investigations.

"Here's an outfit you might need to check on. They too buy illegal arms from the Colonel. It's called Ying-Yang-Black. The address is listed." That was all. No signature, no date. He folded the letter and put it in his pocket.

Two hours later Mark parked the Continental directly in front of the address he wanted, in the fringe area of off-campus apartments around Columbia University. It was racially mixed, with many Orientals, blacks and Puerto Ricans on the street. The time was a little after ten when Mark went up the steps of an old eight-unit apartment house. He knocked and waited. There was no answer. After a pause, Mark turned the knob and went inside. He was in a small hallway, with four doors on the ground floor. He knocked on the first door but got no response. The Penetrator went up the stairs to the next floor and tried the doors there, without result.

Down at the front door again, Mark heard a noise. It sounded like a muffled shout, almost a scream. Quietly he tested the other doors. One led to a basement. He opened it soundlessly and at once was certain the noise had come from below. The Penetrator drew Ava from his hip holster. He had brought it without expecting any real trouble. Cautiously he moved down the steps. At a turn in the stairs he could see the basement below.

Two young Oriental men stood over a naked woman lying on her back, tied to a bench. One man held his hand over her mouth.

The larger of the men tested the sharpness of a fish-filleting knife. It was long and narrow-bladed and looked sharp enough to cut shark hide. He poured lighter fluid on the blade, then set it on fire and began to move the knife toward the girl. Mark aimed and fired, squeezing off the dart-gun trigger softly. The small missile sped through the air and penetrated a quarter of an inch into the man's chest. He jumped, but had time only to look at the small dart tail before he screamed, dropped the knife and clutched his chest.

The special juice in the dart was compounded to do two jobs. First, to inject a muscle spasm agent into the tissue and produce instantaneous and debilitating muscle cramps, preventing any further coordinated action. The cramps lasted for ten seconds, after which the second effect took over. The sodium pentothal and M-99 tranquilizer solutions knocked out the victim and held him under for about fifteen minutes.

It worked exactly as it was supposed to. Mark thumbed a new round into the dart gun and slid it into his other hand.

"Freeze, mister, right there. Don't twitch or you'll get it like your buddy did."

The second youth's back was to Mark. He remained motionless as the Penetrator came down the stairs. Mark watched him critically, then pushed him against the wall and frisked him, turning up a switchblade.

When he looked at the woman, he saw with a jolt that she was Joanna Tabler. She blinked, then smiled through emerging tears.

"Nice you could drop by," Joanna said.

He cut her loose and found her clothes, keeping a watch on the second Chinese.

Joanna dried tears of relief, and sighed. "Why is it I always seem to be naked when I'm around you?"

"Fate," he said. He motioned the student to lie on the bench. Quickly he tied down his legs, then bound him securely around his throat so that the least struggle would tighten the ropes and cut off his air.

Mark picked up the knife and the can of lighter fluid.

"This really work?" he asked the Chinese.

"Hell, we were just scaring her, honest to god!"

Mark poured lighter fluid on the blade until it dripped, then lit it and let the dripping balls of fire land on the youth's shirt front. Mark ripped off the shirt and heard gasps of surprise as the flame balls splattered on the hairless chest. They burned so quickly there was hardly a sensation of heat. Lighter fluid burns that way.

Mark brought the burning knife lower and sliced a groove across the boy's upper chest. The blade bit in only an eighth of an inch, but behind it the knife left a trail of burning lighter fluid and bubbling blood.

The Chinese screamed.

"No, Henry," Joanna said. She had just slid into her bra and was adjusting her breasts in the cups. "He didn't hurt me."

Mark glanced up at her with a steely, deadly gaze that made her look away.

"Are you part of Black Gold?" Mark asked the whimpering student. New screams filled the room. Mark covered the youth's mouth with his hand and repeated the question. The flames died on the boy's chest.

"No, dammit. We're not Black Gold."

"Why did you kidnap Miss Tabler?"

"Go to hell."

Mark squirted lighter fluid into the slice in the bare chest, and struck a match. "Why, son? Tell me."

Fearful, shocked eyes stared at the lighted match as if unable to turn away.

"Okay, just don't light that stuff. She was asking questions, that's why. She wanted to know where we got some dynamite we needed. We don't know how she found out we had it."

"Where is the black part of Ying-Yang-Black?"

"No niggers. Black means death, man."

"You sure?" Mark lit another match from the first one and moved it lower.

"Yeah, man, I'm sure."

Mark saw all the signs of a lie. The match touched the end of the bloody furrow and the flame shot along the eight-inch river. The Chinese youth screamed again. Joanna turned away, slipping quickly into the rest of her clothes, ignoring her pantyhose.

Mark's hand muffled the screams. At last he leaned down and blew out the fire. It would leave a deep, angry scar for as long as the man lived.

"Are you part of Black Gold?"

Tears worked down the Chinese's cheeks. He twisted in pain; he could hardly speak. "Yes, dammit.

131

We work with them. Recruit, help raise money . . ."

Then it was too late for any more questions. The Chinese passed out.

Mark picked up the youth who had been tranquilized and headed up the stairs. Joanna came right behind him. They got the Chinese into Mark's car, ignoring two curious onlookers. Then they drove away.

"Take him to my apartment," Joanna said. "We can bring him in the back way."

"I need to sit down and reason with this boy," Mark said.

"Of course, but you can't reason your way around one of the Algonquin's Round Tables."

11

TWO MILLION QUICK KILL

Twenty minutes later they had the man in the kitchen of Joanna's modest apartment in the Seventies. He was coming around. Mark tied his hands behind him and rolled him on his stomach. He pulled up his legs, bent the knees and hog-tied ankles to wrists, pulling the ropes tight. Then, using a small nylon line, he made a series of loops around the youth's ankles and his throat. The more the boy struggled, the tighter the slip knot pulled. Two or three violent struggling minutes and he would choke himself to death.

The Penetrator waited until his captive began to regain consciousness, then threw a glass of cold water in his face. The Chinese groaned.

"What the hell? Hey, where am I? What's going on?" He kept asking questions, but Mark was sure he knew exactly what his situation was, and that it was hopeless.

Mark squatted beside him on the kitchen floor.

"Now, fish-face, we talk. I ask the questions. You answer me or I start cutting off your air supply, you understand?" Mark gave the man's hands an upward yank and the cord around his throat tightened until he gasped. Mark loosened it so he could breathe again.

"Now you get the idea. What's your name?"

"Billy Ching."

"Your buddy told us about your Black Gold connection. Have you talked to Abdul Daley lately?"

"Who?"

Joanna took the rope which tied the man's hands and pulled upward on it. Again Billy Ching gasped for breath, his face slowly turning purple.

"Abdul Daley." Mark repeated, then signaled for Joanna to loosen the slip knot. Mark was surprised at the woman's reaction, and her ability to use force. It was the response of a trained, seasoned intelligence agent.

Ching sputtered, gasping for breath.

"Haven't seen him for two days, maybe three."

"What's your connection?"

"That's it, a connection. He needs the H, and he needs us to supply it. I work with the girl sometimes."

"What girl?"

"Any girl, man."

Mark hit him in the face with the back of his hand.

"Go ahead, snuff me. See how much information you get from a corpse."

Mark's hands swung simultaneously this time, not as hard as he could swing, but hard. His open palms clapped the sides of Ching's head, directly over his ears, sending two massive pressure waves against his eardrums. At least one of them ruptured.

"Lousy bastard!" Billy screamed, tears seeping down his cheeks.

Mark watched him fight the pain. He knew Ching could hear him.

"Do you know Soo Lin?"

Ching's head snapped up at the name. Mark had his answer to that one.

"Where is the headquarters of Black Gold?"

"Try and find it."

Mark nodded at Joanna, who pulled on Ching's hand rope. Ching gagged.

"Where is it, Ching?"

Silence.

Mark looked at Joanna, who tugged at the cord again. Once more the nylon loop tightened until Ching nearly passed out. At the last moment the Penetrator loosened the knot. This wasn't the way to deal with Ching.

Mark let the blade on his right wrist slide down into his hand. Ching blinked. He couldn't put his head down; he had to hold it as high as he could in order to keep breathing. The position was extremely difficult to maintain for long, and Ching was tiring. Mark ran the knife delicately along Ching's upper lip, barely scratching the skin.

"The death of a thousand slashes, is that a familiar term to you, Mr. Ching?"

Dark eyes looked up at him, hatred boiling from them.

"You won't kill me, I know that."

Mark took from his pocket one of his blue flint arrowheads. He held it so Ching could see it but Joanna couldn't. The effect was immediate. The defiance melted, the young face lost its aggressive leer, and unguarded fear now mixed with wonder.

"My god. You would kill me! I mean, I'm not about to take the count for them other sons of bitches. Soo Lin isn't too sure they're playing square with us anyway, and . . ."

"Billy, where is the headquarters?"

"Up on 172nd Street. An old apartment house they bought and took over a year ago. It's called the Wayward Arms." He was shivering now and sweating too. He looked up. "God, can you take this rope off my throat?"

"You heard how they bombed the TV broadcasting cables. What else are they planning?"

"Planning? They don't tell me. All I know is they had three hits set up, two days apart." He frowned. "Now what the hell was the last one? I never figured they'd pull off either one." He thought a moment. "Damn, something to do with the water supply for all of Manhattan."

"Water? Were they going to cut it off? Blow up the lines? Contaminate it? What?"

"I can't remember. Soo Lin said something about the stuff would be in soon from mainland China. She said a lot of people would be surprised—the ones who lived."

"If it's something coming in, it must be poison or atomic, or something more deadly," Joanna said. Mark nodded.

He cut the cord looped around Ching's throat, then sliced the bindings holding his hands and feet. The Chinese rolled on his back.

"Anything else you can tell us, Ching?"

The Chinese looked up at the towering dark figure above him and shivered. God, he'd read the morning papers. This was the guy who was the damn Penetrator, the freelance hit man who clobbered that heroin drop in Chinatown and wiped out Abdul's paint-shop crew. He tried to think. He'd tell this cat anything he knew.

"Nothing else I can say. But watch that Wayward Arms place. It looks easy, but I hear it's set up like a fort. Machine guns with interlocking fields of fire, military discipline inside, and plenty of loaded weapons and men to use them. But the place is all black guys. They wouldn't even let me take a look inside. It certainly isn't going to be easy if you plan on shooting your way in there."

Mark pulled Ching up by his shirt front and stood him on unsteady feet.

"Kid, if any of this isn't for real, if you laid just one lie on me, I'm gonna come find you and cut out your tongue and have myself a sandwich while you watch me eat it. You savvy?"

"Yeah, but it's all true. So help me."

"Nobody will be able to kid, if it isn't."

A half hour later, Mark dropped Ching off in the Chinese section. He drove uptown, then pulled into a side street and tried to think it through. What he needed was a good look inside that fortress before he moved in for a killing blow. But could he manage a soft assault, a quiet little recon? He thought of going back to the hotel and putting on his black disguise, but he rejected that.

He drove up Broadway a few blocks until he found a place to eat. He devoured a steak, and with some trouble got the side dishes he wanted: a big tossed green salad with a bowl of roquefort dressing, plenty of baby green peas, baked potato with chives and sour cream, and a quart of milk.

When he came out of the restaurant he decided he had to take a chance with a soft hit. He got in the car and drove up Broadway toward 172nd Street. The radio came on and announced the latest Black Gold coup. New York City's finest had failed again to nab the extortionists in a money drop. Mark listened as he drove. Confusion was the primary factor in the story, but half an hour later the details started coming.

The police had been ordered to bring the three million dollars' payoff money in used twenties to upper Broadway in a Honda Civic auto. A radio message directed to the midget driver of the Honda told him to wheel up Broadway and keep going. Police units scrambled, following and covering the little car. It looked easy.

A hundred and fifty units, including two choppers, were on the chase. They paralleled the Honda, followed it, and even preceded it. The car passed Columbia University, then drove on past the George Washington Bridge.

When the Honda neared the Harlem River, a radio message told the driver to turn into the Baker Field football stadium parking lot, roll down both front windows of the car and then run for his life. He did exactly that.

Before the nearest police units could close up the safety gap they had left for the car, an Alouette Lama helicopter swept in from the river and hovered low over the car. One black man jumped out and fastened a four-point pickup sling under the Honda, and within thirty seconds the car and the chopper were both airborne.

When the first police unit skidded to a stop, the French-built chopper was already out of pistol range and heading for New Jersey. Police choppers were called in, but since they had been ordered to hang back a mile to avoid being spotted, it took them almost two minutes to reach the spot, then more time to trail and find the chopper.

On board the Alouette, the black men worked fast. A rope ladder was lowered from the chopper's door. A man climbed down and wormed through the Honda's open window. Inside the car he quickly attached a rope to the three suitcases full of money, which were promptly hoisted up into the machine.

The man then climbed up the rope ladder into the Alouette, and as soon as he gained the helicopter cabin, the Honda and the slings were dropped into the middle of the Hudson River.

New York police notified New Jersey law enforcement officials about the heist and the helicopter, but somewhere in the New Jersey system the call went to the wrong office, and by the time the officers who could be of some help were notified, almost twenty minutes had elapsed. By then it was far too late.

When the N.Y.P.D. choppers spotted the Alouette it was over New Jersey, but they pursued. They were lighter and faster, and soon closed the gap. The Alouette drove them off with two dozen shots from a long-range weapon, later found to be a 300 Weatherby Magnum rifle. One police chopper was hit in the engine and made a forced landing. The second helicopter took one round with no damage. The pilot was

139

ordered to hang back and observe, reporting to Jersey police where the rig landed.

The Black Gold Alouette eluded the N.Y.P.D. aircraft by flying low around buildings and groves of trees, and at last landed undetected in a small clearing. A man ran out with a winch, hooked it onto the chopper and pulled it out of sight under some big trees.

Police said after the extortionists hid the helicopter they had only to get into two waiting cars and drive away. The New Jersey police had arrived on the scene after they left. They did establish that the Alouette had been reported stolen the week before from the Teterboro Airport.

Mark listened to the wailing and gnashing of teeth of the radio commentator, then turned him off. Black Gold had to be stopped. It was mandatory that he make the soft probe now. He couldn't go in on a full-scale assault without some idea of the layout, the firepower.

He drove up Broadway to 96th Street and took one of the Riverside Park turnouts. When he spotted a deserted area, he parked and opened the trunk. He checked over the first suitcase and selected the Hi-Standard .22 automatic and the matching silencer. He also took a spare magazine and slid it into his pocket. The Penetrator left the dart gun in the suitcase and snuggled the .22 into the hip holster. His wrist knife was back in place. On a hunch he put one of the new-style white phosphorous grenades in his pocket.

After thinking about it again, he picked up the dart gun and pushed the muzzle into his belt. It might be handy to have along in case he needed to put down some civilian without wasting him.

140

The Penetrator locked the trunk and drove off, ready now for his probe of the fortress.

The apartment complex he was looking for on 172nd was old. It had degenerated into a slum. The building had four stories. Only a few of the windows had curtains. No children played in front of this building, no oldsters chatted on the steps, and no women moved in and out with strollers. It covered half the front of the block and had one large entranceway with steps. A sleepy-looking black youth lounged there, apparently killing time, but actually serving as a bright-eyed lookout, missing nothing that happened on the street.

Mark drove on past, then eased to the curb a block further on, behind a Cadillac. He put on an old hat, scarf and sunglasses. He didn't own a topcoat, but now he needed one.

Mark walked slowly toward the fortress. He knew the black lookout had seen him as soon as he crossed the street, so he put on the whole act. He stopped and looked up at the street sign, then walked on, shaking his head. He had the dart gun out and under his jacket as he walked.

"Hey, man, I'm looking for Alford Street. It up here?" Mark asked as he came near the youth.

"Cut out, man. I ain't no damn information booth," the kid said.

Mark shot him with the dart, caught him before he could roll down the steps, and carried him upward. He pushed the guard against the side of the building at the top of the steps and ran to the entrance. Inside, just in back of the door, an eight-foot-high wall of sandbags had been built. He peered around and saw two blacks moving away down the hall.

The Penetrator waited till it was clear, then ran lightly for the stairs and went up them three steps at a time. He paused, crouching, before showing himself on the second level; but the hall was empty. Mark spotted an open door to what looked like an empty room. He checked it, then slipped past the door and closed it behind him. He snapped the night lock. The room was set up for a class, with chalkboard, ten chairs and a partially disassembled .30 caliber Browning automatic rifle on a table.

At the rear window he could see into the courtyard below. It was over a hundred feet square, and empty of any plantings or furniture. The building completely surrounded the court. Guards holding small machine guns over their shoulders stood at the four entrances to the court.

In the area, Mark saw three crews running through 81 mm mortar practice. First a baseplate man ran up and slammed the plate into the ground. A man with the barrel ran up next, put the ball joint into the base socket and twisted the barrel half a turn, locking it in. Then the gunner charged up with the bipod, opened the clamp, put it around the barrel and fastened it. At once he began moving the bipod, adjusting the elevation and crossing handles, sighting in on the aiming stake ten yards ahead of him.

It was basic training all over again, only this "army" wore strange all-black uniforms. Mark checked the firepower and frowned. He needed to find out what kind of poison Black Gold had and how it was going to be used—and the Chinese youth had said he had only two days. But he wasn't equipped for a hard hit against this much firepower. He took the silencer from his pocket and screwed it on the Hi-Standard. The combination made a potent high-penetration killing weapon, and one that made little more noise than the snap of his fingers. He pushed a new round in the dart gun and returned it to his belt.

The Penetrator held the silenced automatic under his coat as he left the safety of the room and moved down the hall. A man yelled from behind Mark, and he turned in time to see a rifle being leveled at him from thirty feet away. Mark shot silently as he turned. The man with the rifle screamed as the small slug slanted upward through his chest, knocking him down the stairs.

Mark ran for the nearest stairway, but boots clattering on the steps stopped him. He retreated and jumped into a room, softly easing the door closed.

He had not checked the room in his rush, and now he felt the presence of someone behind him. As he turned he saw Soo Lin, a smile on her small face. Behind her sat ten black-uniformed men. On a table lay a Chinese automatic weapon, a burp gun. It was partially disassembled.

Soo Lin laughed as she swung up another such weapon from her shoulder. It was pointed directly at him, and her finger rested on its hair trigger.

"Drop your weapon, Mr. Penetrator. Your killing days are over."

Mark Hardin looked at her, and as he did he brought up the .22 Hi-Standard. If he was buying it he could at least take her with him.

12

CHINESE DEATH EXPERIMENT

There was something wrong with the woman's smile. It came across too casual, overplayed. By the time the Penetrator's Hi-Standard was up he knew what it was. She held only a demonstration machine gun; it wasn't loaded.

Mark fired a silent round into the disassembled weapon on the table, scattering the parts.

"Yours is unloaded, Soo Ling. You might as well put it down."

A man in the back of the room rushed for the rear door. Mark swung his arm and the silenced automatic coughed, sending a slug through the back of the running man's head. The blackshirt skidded forward as the bullet fragments inside his skull turned three vital brain centers into pulp, snuffing his life in half a second.

The Penetrator turned his weapon toward the woman. "Is there a loaded magazine for that chatter gun?"

She shouted at him in Chinese and threw the machine gun at him. He caught it and scowled. "Speak English, Soo Lin. I know you can."

Another man had crept toward the back door. Mark called for him to stop; but he didn't. Mark blasted a high-speed slug into his side. He flopped once on the floor and lay still. Four of Mark's ten shots were gone. Two more men bolted for the front door, and he cut them down, hitting both in the legs with three shots.

Mark ran for the table and jerked open a drawer. Soo Lin screamed at him, threw a small knife which missed, and then ran for the door. Mark's pistol came up quickly and his finger tightened on the trigger, then relaxed. He still couldn't shoot a woman. It was one of the Victorian standards that had never been conditioned out of him.

Soo Lin jerked open the door and ran out. He heard her screaming her way down the hall. Mark found another drawer, scooped up a loaded magazine for the chatter toy, jammed it home and chambered a round. He swung it toward the cowering black recruits, then charged into the hall. He fired in five-round bursts as he charged the stairs, going down. Small arms fired back. He killed three men on the stairs as he swept down and raced toward the front door.

Two burp guns chattered in front of him, slugs denting the walls and ceiling. He darted into a room, wondering why one of the slugs hadn't found him. Mark pulled the white phosphorous grenade from his pocket, leaped to the door, pulled the pin and thew the bomb into the hall. At least he was on the first floor. He heard the pop of the Willy Peter grenade in the hall. That would slow up anyone who wanted to come into this room. Now he ran to the window, but it was fastened shut.

With the butt of the burp gun he smashed out the glass and looked into the street. He could smell the phosphorous now in the hall, hear the crackling of burning wood. A fire was just the ticket now. Mark leaned out the window, stepped over the shards of glass and jumped. He rolled as he hit, holding the gun close to his body. He rolled twice and came up running, pounding down the sidewalk toward his car.

One man yelled behind him. No one chased him. He saw one man come out of the building but he didn't give chase. A window broke behind him on the second floor of the big building and he heard the snarl of a handgun, but already he was out of effective range. A block away he looked back and saw smoke coming from a broken window. A fire alarm would sound soon, and the black-shirted warriors inside would have their hands full hiding illegal weapons before the fire department arrived. Idly he wondered if a property owner could refuse to allow a city fire department to enter his property and put out a fire in his building. He wasn't going to wait to find out.

Mark jogged the last half-block to the Continental, got into the front and stuffed the burp gun out of sight under the seat. He drove away from the burning building for six blocks, then turned and headed toward it. He could now see smoke climbing into the sky.

As his car approached the building, he was stopped by a young fireman who had just dropped off a fire truck which was backing toward the blaze, spinning off a main line as it went. Two more trucks

146

whined up, and men scattered to their work. He saw fire break out of the front of the old wooden building as he turned down the cross-street.

Mark laughed dryly as he moved back toward the Algonquin. Not bad for a simple little soft recon.

He stopped at a Broadway newsstand and picked up the new editions of the newspapers. The Penetrator was again splashed over the front pages, along with a bulletin about the three-million dollar hijacking with the chopper. The mayor had held a news conference about the problems of the city, and had listed the Penetrator as one of the biggest. Reporters asked why, since the Penetrator had killed only dope pushers and wanted criminals. The mayor was firm in his stand that a killer was a killer, and had to be brought to justice.

Again there were summaries of the activities of the Penetrator in other cities. One paper had a blown-up photo of a blue flint arrowhead sticking out of the chest of the dead heroin pusher.

Mark drove again. What he needed were a few hours to do some advance planning, and to see what he could find out about shipments from mainland China. The more he thought about it, the more he reasoned that the Black Gold shipment could only be one of two items: an atomic bomb, or some type of poison. Then a chilling thought came through. It didn't have to be a simple poison. It might just as well be a culture, some type of germ, something from the bacteriological warfare book of dirty tricks. The thought made him drive faster through traffic back to 44th Street. He decided he'd have to give Mr. Wong another call.

When Mark checked his box at the Algonquin,

there was a message. It was in a neat feminine hand and said simply, "Call me." There was a telephone number. He went to his room and placed the call. The phone on the other end sounded only half a ring before someone took it.

"Yes?"

"I'm calling you. I got your message."

"Good," the woman's voice said. Then he was sure it was Joanna Tabler.

"I've set up a meeting at two-thirty and I want you to come. Mr. Lee Wong will be present, and Police Lieutenant Arthur Chuchulski, as well as some other important people. It ties in with your Abdul case."

Mark checked his watch. It was almost two.

"Where's the meeting?"

"My office. This is my private line number if you want to remember it."

"I'll be there. I need to see Mr. Wong."

He hung up, wondering what Joanna's tie was with Wong. He'd find out in half an hour.

Mark took a taxi to the Diogenes offices. He was the last one to arrive. There were no introductions. One man present was the mayor of New York City. The room was crowded with a dozen other men. The meeting began as Joanna, dressed in a neatly tailored suit, stood.

"Gentlemen, we're here for a serious matter. I should set the scene by saying that during an investigation our firm discovered a circumstance which we now find leads directly to Black Gold. This makes it a police matter, which is why they are represented. I thought Mr. Wong might give us some background."

The small man stood. "The Chinese population in

our city has been threatened, pressured, gouged. Two good men have been murdered, and now a strange new threat comes at us from the mainland of China. We in the Chinese community feel partly responsible, since we did not silence this evil, this cancer, in our own way months ago, when the danger first appeared. Some of us preferred to go into hiding instead."

Wong stared at Mark. "We were wrong. Now it is a fight for principle. For some it is a fight for survival. Today in the Bronx Zoo three giraffes in a special enclosure died. Veterinarians at once determined the cause of death. I think one of them should report to you."

Dr. Lewis Jarbowski stood. The strain on him was obvious. One eye moved with a spasmodic tic. He clasped his hands in front of him, then in back. At last he folded his arms.

"Today we lost three rare and valuable animals. Our conclusion is that they were deliberately exposed to a malady that is so deadly, so dangerous, and so horrendous that we had four outside specialists certify that our diagnosis was correct before we notified the authorities. Now we are certain.

"The cause of death is a submicroscopic virus that it extremely difficult to detect. It has a multiplicative power of some yet unknown pattern, but it is explosively prolific. It is thought for sure now that this is one virus that can live and multiply outside of living cells.

"The only known outbreak of any serious nature of this virus was in a small mountain village in Peru about twenty-five years ago. A hundred and eighty-seven residents of the village perished within two hours. Two teams of investigators sent there died almost at once. The village was then sealed off by the government and the World Health Organization, and the whole village was destroyed with saturation napalm bombing. Homes, bodies, vehicles, churches, animals, every physical item was burned, then totally burned again. A third saturation napalm bombing was used to be sure that every trace of the virus had been destroyed. For two weeks, hourly spray applications of the most deadly germicidal nerve gases known to man were spread over the village and a surrounding area a mile in diameter."

There was a murmur of surprise, and whispers.

"That outbreak was stopped," Dr. Jarbowski continued. "There was an unconfirmed report that some of the virus was used in the Korean War by the Chinese, but it was never proved. We understand from U.S. Intelligence that the only known supply of active X-447 is in the People's Republic of China.

"Our three giraffes died of X-447. Their bodies have been cremated where they fell. The water they drank from has been pumped into lead bottles and flown to one of the deepest coal mines in West Virginia and sealed off at the bottom of a shaft. The entire zoo is closed for a month. The giraffe compound has been burned repeatedly until nothing could live in it. This virus can be either water- or air-borne, and can spread effectively by either method." He sighed. "That's about my part of it. I think Police Commissioner McNeely should take over."

The portly commissioner did not stand. He looked around the room and shook his head. "Today has been disastrous for our city. Now we have received a private and top secret message from Black Gold.

Everyone in this room is sworn to secrecy. Nothing that is said here can be repeated outside this room to anyone not now present. If it gets out to the press, we could have a panic on our hands that would result in hundreds of thousands of deaths right here in Manhattan."

He paused and looked around at each person there.

"Today, Black Gold told us that they were responsible for the animal deaths in the Bronx Zoo, and that if we do not meet their demands, the entire water supply of all of Manhattan will be contaminated with X-447. If that happens there will be absolutely no way we can prevent the deaths of at least two million people within minutes. They gave us twenty-four hours to reply.

"Their demands are simple. They demand the unconditional resignation of the mayor, the City Council and all of the commissioners, and the installation of Black Gold as the legal ruling junta of New York City within a week. As a good faith gesture, they also demand the payment of one hundred million dollars in cash before midnight tomorrow!"

13

HARD SITE BLAST-IN

The shocked silence lasted for almost sixty seconds. The mayor stood, but for once he couldn't find any words. He made a helpless gesture with one hand and sat down.

Lt. Chuchulski started the action. He suggested an emergency task force to search out Black Gold. It would include all law-enforcement agencies, U.S. government agents, and the New York National Guard units. Anyone with personal information about Black Gold was asked to talk with Chulchulski now. Mr. Chang moved to him at once.

Mark looked at Joanna. She caught his signal and walked toward him. He spoke in low tones.

"Don't tell them about Abdul, not yet. I'm paying him a visit as soon as it gets dark. If you hear nothing from me by nine o'clock tonight, call the police and tell them everything you know."

"Henry, you can't go in there alone."

"It's the only way. It's got to be a surprise, before

they can move, hide or spread around that package that must have arrived from China."

"You think it's up there?"

"That's where I'd keep it if I were running the game."

She warned him with her eyes just before the man touched his shoulder. Mark turned and looked into the grim face. This was the cop.

"Yes, Lieutenant, can we help you?" Joanna asked.

"Input. I need to know everything about Black Gold."

"You already have my report, including all names and locations we suspected."

Mark studied the man. He was serious, efficient, probably a good cop. He would have been on the take for a while, then wised up or moved out of vice. But Mark wouldn't trust him to make an assault on a pillbox filled with pot-smoking Viet Cong whores.

Chuchulski stared at Mark.

"I'm from out of town," Mark said. "Joanna thought I might be able to help, but I don't see how."

"I'm on track of one more item that might help," Joanna said. "I'll be able to tie it down by nine tonight. It may be nothing, and then again it could lead us right into their headquarters."

The cop seemed satisfied. He moved on.

A half-hour later everyone had left the office except Mark and Joanna. Another strategy meeting was to be held in an hour in the mayor's office. The governor would be there.

"Did you see our mayor?" Joanna asked. "I never

thought I'd see him without words. The poor man is terrified."

"True. Like anybody the first time he goes into combat. I thought he was going to dirty his drawers." Mark stared out the big windows at the late-afternoon sunshine. Did he have to wait until dark? He decided he did. That would make it one hell of a lot simpler. But could he afford the time? He had another question that had to be answered first.

"Joanna. Just how does your illegal arms deal tie in with Black Gold?"

"They used illegal arms, that C-4 plastic explosive . . ."

Mark shook his head. "That doesn't do it for me."

"Henry, any other reasons are confidential between me and my client."

"Could that client be from Washington? Have you ever heard of the Industrial Relations Research Section located in the Department of Labor at 14th and Constitution Avenues?"

"Henry, we're in investigations, not public relations," she said evenly.

He watched her closely. "I'll tell Dan that next time I see him." She hadn't moved, hadn't tensed, frozen, gasped; no eyelid trembled, no lips moved, so she was either very good or had no contact at all with Dan Griggs in the Justice Department. Mark gave a little sigh of relief. But soon she would know that he was involved with the Penetrator. The arrowheads tonight would tie that up for her. He shrugged. He couldn't remain completely anonymous forever, not if he expected to do any good.

Mark reached out and pulled her gently toward him. He held her close, aware of the soft scent of her hair, the faint tingle of perfume from behind her ears. He had no idea what the name of it was, but it smelled beautiful. Then a darting memory stopped him. Again he saw Andrea Hughes, and remembered how she had been tortured and raped and brutally killed simply because she had met him once, not because she was involved in the bloody Las Vegas showdown. That was when he had promised himself never to get involved again with a girl.

Mark pushed her away from him, turned and walked quickly to the door.

"Henry? What in the world? Was it something I said?"

He shook his head, the vision of Andrea's torn, mutilated body hitting him full force.

"No, Joanna, it's not you. It's me. Forget you ever met me." He turned and charged through the door.

Mark hurried to the street and grabbed a taxi. He got out in front of the Algonquin. Upstairs in his room he checked his weapons. This would be a one-man assault and he wanted to be well enough equipped to have a 60-40 chance of coming out alive.

First he looked in the Yellow Pages and called three helicopter charter services. At last he chose one, Hel Air Copters Ltd., and reserved a two-man chopper to be at the midtown heliport at 6:30 that evening. It would be totally dark by then.

Next he turned to his weapons. He would wear an Air Force-type flight suit of thin nylon and utlize the pockets. In the top one would go the Hi-Standard model .22, and beside it the silencer. His trusty .45 Commander and three loaded clips would be in a second pocket. He looked at the dart gun but decided the Hi-Standard would work for his quiet attacks.

In lower pockets he put three fragmentation grenades —the old M-3 pineapple types—and two of the new white phosphorous grenades.

From the bottom of the suitcase he took out a Uzi submachine gun. As near as he could tell it was the Israeli special model M-67/SS, built especially for the U.S. Secret Service. It had a standard full-barrel silencer, and was used primarily by the service for "under the coat" protection of the president and state dignitaries.

It was a rugged military weapon as well with a 50-round straight magazine feed through the pistol grip at the balance point. A special counter-recoil mechanism minimized the climb when it was fired on full automatic. This model had a three-position firing selector; it could discharge 450 rounds or 600 rounds per minute, or the semiautomatic switch set to fire just one slug for each trigger pull.

The folding stock had been removed from this one, making it look like a long machine pistol. The handy little weapon fired 9 mm parabellum rounds, and was thought by many arms experts to be the best rapid-fire submachine gun in the world. He tied it to a short loop of sash cord so that it swung from his neck at chest level. It was a murderous chattergun for close fighting, and Mark expected the situation to get a little frenetic tonight before the shooting was over.

Before he dressed in the flight gear, Mark checked the phone book and made a call. A small package was delivered to his room. It was a fully operative small beacon, a red blinker, powered by a battery.

He dressed carefully in the flight suit and loaded the pockets, changed into his Cockran paratrooper boots, then double-checked everything. He was ready.

The Penetrator put on a long raincoat of heavy gabardine and looked in the mirror. He looked slightly heavier than before, but certainly not enough to attract attention as he went through the lobby.

At 5:45 Mark called for his car to be brought around. As he waited, he took a look at the medical bag he'd liberated from Abdul Daley at the heroin drop. He estimated that the bag contained about thirty thousand dollars in cash. Mark counted out two stacks of ten hundred-dollar bills, rolled each stack and snapped small rubber bands around both. He put them deep down in his pocket. Before he left his room he took all his jingles and jangles, and all identification, out of his pockets—just as on any intelligence mission.

The Penetrator arrived at the front door of the Algonquin just after his car was delivered. A five-dollar tip to the car chaser kept him happy. Mark got in and drove to 12th Avenue, then down to 30th Street. The heliport was right next to the Hudson River. He parked where he could watch the Hel Air copters in operation. Precisely at 6:30 he walked past the high fence into the glare of lights and identified himself.

The pilot who motioned him toward a Hughes 300 chopper looked about twenty-five. They both got into the bird, and put on belts. Mark handed the pilot one of the rolls of bills. The young man flicked through it and whistled. He looked quickly at Mark.

"We only charge a hundred thirty an hour. You sure this is all on the level, know what I mean? I don't want to get involved in any kind of a robbery, you know, that kind of thing."

"Nothing like that, man, no sweat. Hey, you fly in 'Nam?"

The pilot nodded.

"Good, I put in a couple of years there too. All we got here is one little vertical assault, very quiet going in, but I can't guarantee how quiet I'll come out. There might be some shooting." Mark saw the pilot's quick look. "But if there is, it will be nothing that the N.Y.P.D. didn't wish they could be doing."

"Shooting, huh? But no robbery. Do you think I look that stupid?"

"Scrub the mission right now, you want to."

"Wait a minute—you a cop? A federal of some kind?"

"Not really." Mark pulled one of the blue flint arrowheads from his pocket and gave it to the pilot.

"Goddam!" he said. "You mean you're that . . ."

"Like I say, you can scrub it right now. I've got a little pickup job to do, some kind of a container these cats are trying to mix in with the water."

"Germ warfare?"

"Without a war. I go in and get it, you help me get it to the cops and the feds."

The pilot laughed and started the countdown. "Hell, this is gonna be a ball, know what I mean? I'll put you exactly where you want to be and come back exactly when you want me to be there!"

"Good boy."

They were off the ground before the pilot spoke again.

"The bread?"

"Yours, all thousand of it. Flight pay, hazard pay.

When we get back I've got another roll of the same amount. One thousand dollars. You pay my charter bill and any damage to the rig, and the rest of it's your gravy."

The chopper pilot grinned. Mark suggested he follow the Hudson upstream and keep low.

On the short flight, the Penetrator stripped off the raincoat. The pilot looked away when he saw the submachine gun. Mark outlined what he wanted done. The pilot would drop Mark off, then come back to the same spot exactly fourteen minutes after lift-off. The chopper was to wait not more than three minutes, and if Mark didn't come he should pull back and watch the beacon. If the beacon went off for 30 seconds, then came back on, that was the pickup signal.

They had a little trouble finding 172nd Street. Then the Penetrator recognized it by a small commercial complex, and the chopper flew over and settled down toward the rear roof of the quadrangle building. Mark opened the door and dropped two feet to the roof, set out the beacon and waved the pilot away.

He made sure the beacon was flashing correctly and could be seen only from the sky, then moved to the edge of the roof and looked into the courtyard. It was dark. He heard some movement below but couldn't identify it. Night problems?

Since he had met no opposition on the roof, he was sure now that Black Gold put most of its defenses on the ground floor to repel a conventional ground-level thrust. So far he'd guessed right.

He ran for the nearest hatch cover that looked like an entryway. The first wouldn't move, but a dozen feet over he lifted up the second one easily. Below was light and a ladder leading down to the end of a hall. He dropped down quickly and quietly. As he did, a door opened and a young black, no more than fourteen, walked into the hall.

Mark's big .45 Commander was out as he grabbed the youth by the shirt front and propelled him back into the room he had just left. It was empty. Mark slammed the boy against the closed door.

"Where's Abdul Daley's room, his pad?"

The youth, too scared to speak, rolled his eyes and shook his head.

"Where, dammit, or I'm gonna blow your head right off those black shoulders." He lifted the muzzle to the boy's head.

"Second floor, back. Right below here. But there's a guard."

Mark's left-hand karate chop smashed down before the youth saw it, catching him at the side of the neck and jolting him into unconsciousness. Mark ripped off the boy's shirt, tied him hand and foot, and gagged him.

The Penetrator eased out the door, cleared the hall and made it all the way to the stairs before a man coming the other way shouted. Mark had switched to the Hi-Standard .22 now with the silencer firmly in place. He fired, and the black-shirted man looked surprised as the small slug bored between his ribs, blasting a deadly hole in his heart. Mark let him lie where he fell.

He moved carefully down the stairs, then down another flight toward the second floor. His whole strategy was to find Abdul, capture the X-447 as quietly as he could, then get out any way he could. He'd

160

use the frags, the WP and his .45 automatic then; damn the noise. But first he had to have the small black man. All Mark knew was the police description—five feet tall, and given to long, ducktailed haircuts. It should be enough.

He slowed as he neared the second-floor landing. The stairs were not enclosed. He stopped at the landing and peered around the banister. Two men guarded a door halfway down the hall.

There was no easy way to get at them. No casually walking up and smashing them. It had to be long-range. He decided not to use the WP grenade. Instead he took the Hi-Standard and checked the silencer. He sighted down on the closest guard and fired. It took two whispering slugs to put down the man. When the first man collapsed, he sent one round into the chest of the second guard, who sighed and fell straight down.

The Penetrator ran ahead as quietly as he could and tried the guarded door. It was locked. He dropped a blue flint arrowhead on the closest body, then kicked the flimsy door down with his heavy right boot. The frame splintered on the second kick and the door swung inward.

Abdul wasn't there. It was a bedroom, lavishly decorated with a big round bed in the middle and mirrors on the ceiling. A naked girl sat up, evidently just coming awake. Mark recognized Soo Lin as she dove swiftly for a pillow. She threw the cushion at him and grabbed the gun under it.

Mark reacted automatically this time. His Hi-Standard coughed quietly from waist level and he saw the flesh of her breast bounce as the lead pellet smashed directly through her left nipple and splattered into her heart. She stared at him in shocked disbelief, then muttered two words in Chinese as she fell backwards across the bed.

Mark tossed a blue flint arrowhead on the bed and scanned the room for a connecting door. There was only one. He opened it a fraction of an inch soundlessly and looked inside.

A man who could only be Abdul Daley lay naked on a bed, surrounded by seven girls in various stages of undress doing wildly erotic dances.

Mark kicked the door open.

"Freeze, all of you!" he roared in his best top sergeant's voice. "I just want Abdul, I won't hurt the rest of you."

It was a scene from a crazy movie. The girls screamed and flew at him in a tortured, violent, animal rage. He waved the gun at them but they didn't even see it. They clawed him, ripped at his clothes, grabbed his hair. They crashed into him, yelling every dirty word they could call up. That was when he saw their glazed eyes, their dilated pupils. He tried to dodge them, realizing they were only sheep, sheep of at least three different races and stoned out of their minds.

But before he could get untangled from them, before he could push them aside and sight in on Abdul, the little man scooted off the bed and, still naked, sprinted through a side door, slamming it after him. For a moment the girls swirled past Mark; then they turned and ran at him again, screaming, long red fingernails poised for attack.

14

THE CRYOGENIC SCREAM

Mark saw his quarry vanish through the far door. At that moment he stopped trying to deal gently with the sheep. He pushed them roughly aside, slamming past and over bodies as he charged for the door. He couldn't afford to let his target get away. The grenades banged his legs as he ran, but he hardly noticed them.

Mark threw open the door, then crouched well to one side against the wall. Two shots blasted through the open space, chest high. He jammed a new clip into the Hi-Standard and leaned into the opening, stitching two slugs into the chest of a black man who rose from behind an overturned table. No one else was in the room.

Mark sprinted to the next door, opened it and ran through, low. Ahead in the hall he saw Abdul, his naked black body galloping hard for the stairs. Abdul was screaming at the top of his voice. Mark fired once over his head, saw him duck down the stairs, and raced after him. A door opened before the Penetrator reached the steps. Mark hit the panel with his shoulder, slamming the heavy door shut. He saw it crush an arm as it slammed, breaking both arm bones. A hand dropped a pistol. A man inside the room screamed and the arm vanished.

Mark surged past, gun waving, and charged down the stairs three steps at a time after Abdul. The stairs went to the first floor, then on down to a basement, and Mark slowed as he came to the last flight of the steps. Two Black Gold soldiers blocked his way. One had a burp gun, the other a rifle. Mark shifted the Hi-Standard to his left hand and took the .45 in his right. He edged around the banister and fired downward, catching the chatter gun man in the chest, driving him against the far wall. The other man fired, splintering wood over Mark's head.

But the big Colt sounded twice more, and the second guard went cartwheeling backwards with two slugs in his head, one smashing his nose to jelly before it slammed on through his skull.

The dead men had been guarding a steel door in the basement. By the time Mark got there it was locked. He fired four slugs into its lock from his .45, jammed a new clip into the handle and kicked the door open. He dove to the side and heard a dozen shots from inside the room.

Mark took one of the M-3 grenades from his zipper pocket, pulled the pin, let the handle flip off and cooked it for two seconds before he tossed the bomb inside the room. Two seconds later it exploded with steel-splintering death. The shock wave billowed out of the room with the punch of a sledgehammer. The roaring crash of the explosion sounded like a dozen thunderclaps. Mark was moving before the sound died. He charged into the room, an automatic in each hand. One man ducked behind a big tank across the thirty-foot storage room.

Mark rolled behind some wooden boxes and surveyed the damage. Three men lay shredded near the center of the room. Another man groaned nearby. Mark heard movement behind the tank. When a man ran for the back door, Mark silenced him with a whisper-quiet shot from his .22, then nailed him with a .45 slug through the spine before he hit the floor.

Mark checked the other bodies, then ran to the door at the far side of the room. He opened it, but drew no more fire. The Penetrator looked in, expecting an ambush. It was the furnace room. Four steps led down to it; there was a mass of tanks and pipes, and a big firebox in the middle. Toward the back, Mark heard someone moving. He charged through the door and down the steps, looking for cover.

Abdul Daley stepped from behind a water tank. He was still naked, but now held a steel bottle two feet long. It was about six inches in diameter and heavily insulated. He had a towel around it and it showed white with frost.

"Stay right there, you honkey bastard," Abdul snarled. "Not another step or I'll blow us all to hell."

He put the bottle down on top of an oil drum and faced Mark. He now had the poise and control of the victor in his voice.

"You dig what I got here dumb-dumb? I got enough germs to wipe out the whole damn city of New York, that's what. All I got to do is open this one little valve and we got germs all over the whole messed up East Coast! Germs or viruses or some damn thing."

Before he finished the sentence, Mark's Colt Commander had tilted up from where he held it by his side. The roar of the .45 caught Abdul by surprise. The big chunk of lead angled upward; a fraction of a second before it hit him, Abdul's mouth sagged open. The 200 grains of lead caught him in the shoulder socket, smashing the cartilage, half-tearing the arm joint apart, and hurling Abdul four feet backwards.

Mark ran to the bottle. It was so cold it gave off a white vapor. He checked a thermometer built into the packing. It showed almost fifteen below zero.

Abdul pushed himself up with his good arm.

"Go ahead, honkey, try to get it out of here. My men'll riddle you, blow you apart, and they'll blast open the bottle too. You'll do my work for me, honkey dumbnuts. It's got to stay cold, stupid. It gets up to twenty degrees over zero, it blows sky high."

Mark checked his watch. Seven minutes had elapsed since he left the chopper, seven to go.

He was still checking the bottle when he saw Abdul struggle to his feet and move toward a valve marked "steam." With the steam hose he could wash down Mark and the bottle and explode the stuff right there in seconds.

Mark grabbed the big bottle and carried it behind a pair of heavy steel support posts, then reached for a white phosphorous grenade. He pulled the pin and let the handle snap off, then tossed it at Abdul.

The pop of the igniting grenade sounded like a small firecracker to Mark behind the posts, as the deadly burning phosphorous granules sprayed the area. Once phosphorous is exposed to the air it begins to burn, and almost nothing can put it out—not water, foam or dirt, and especially not human flesh.

The scream came almost at once. When the last of the WP stopped falling, Mark looked past his steel protection and saw Abdul writhing on the floor. His hands clawed at his throat where dozens of the pellets had imbedded themselves and were burning. A glob of WP had struck his chest and sizzled as it burned through flesh and into bone. One of Abdul's eyes was closed by the sticky, white burning material that had splattered his face.

As Mark watched, Abdul's struggling gradually slowed until his one good hand was barely moving. His wails and shrieks came bubbling one on top of another. The shock of the WP and the physical pain had taken most of his vitality. Now the phosphorous burned into his throat and ruptured one of the carotid arteries. The red floodtide surged down his neck, pooling in other craters caused by the still-burning WP. It was the first time Mark had ever seen human blood boil. He stared at it for a moment, then heard a long sigh. It was a death rattle, the final unconscious act of Abdul's body as the last rush of air escaped his lungs.

Mark pushed a blue flint arrowhead into one of the burn holes and hurried out of the boiler room. Some trash in one corner had caught fire from the WP and flames were eating into the foundations of the wooden structure.

He had to try to get the bottle out to the cops, get it to a refrigerated truck before it went off. There was no way he could hold off the army of Black

Gold men here. He had to fight his way back to the roof and be ready to leave in exactly five minutes. The built-in thermometer on the packing read thirteen below zero. Mark ran.

At the doorway of the outer room he peered into the basement hall. Four men with drawn pistols and rifles hid in doorways between him and the stairs.

Mark put down the bottle and chambered a round into the Uzi, then with the weapon on full automatic he sprayed the hall with lead. He switched the Uzi to semi-automatic fire and picked off the one remaining enemy alive in the hall, then let the machine gun swing from his neck while he ran with the bottle. He held the container over one shoulder and grabbed his .45 with the other hand. Mark got up the first stairway with no trouble, then saw a cluster of defenders in the first-floor hall.

He stopped just out of sight of them, took out his last WP grenade and threw it down the hall, watching it spray, scattering the gunners with the fiery pellets. He hurried up the stairs to the second floor in the confusion and took only one wild protesting shot.

Mark made it to the third floor, then had a running fire fight with two gunmen who knew what they were doing. At last he put the bottle down and turned the Uzi to full automatic. He jumped into the hall and hosed down the two doorways and half the hall. One of the men fell from a doorway. Mark saw he wore a green beret; probably a Vietnam vet. The other gunner crumpled into the hall, screaming in pain. Mark dashed for the top floor and made it. He found no opposition there. He climbed the ladder and lifted off the hatch cover, then took up the heavy cryogenic bottle and pushed it over the edge onto the roof.

Then, before he could move, a small handgun edged out from a partly-opened door ten feet down the hall. For one terrible moment time froze. He was dead. There was no defense, no time to move, to draw his own weapon, no hope that the gunner could miss him at that range. Suddenly he noticed the hand was small, slender, a woman's hand, with polish on the nails.

Then the moment disintegrated into normal time and the gun went off. Mark felt the slug hit his chest, experienced the crushing pain as it slammed into him like a thunderbolt. He nearly lost his hold on the rungs of the ladder. There was no second shot. The hand was shaking. He watched it pull the gun in and heard the door lock. He had not dropped off the ladder, so he knew he wasn't dead. He hadn't felt pain like that since his last wound in 'Nam.

It coursed through every nerve-ending in his body, setting each one afire with searing agony. His lungs throbbed and burned. No! God no. Not a bullet through a lung! He didn't have time for that kind of hospital treatment. He had a job to finish.

He used both arms to slowly, painfully pull himself inch by inch up the rungs, until he could fall over the top of the opening onto the roof.

He knew his legs were still showing below. Anyone could blast him off at the waist with a chopper. He couldn't reach any of his weapons. Sticky, wet blood soaked into his nylon suit from his chest. For a moment he wondered if he were dying.

Maybe he was already dead and didn't know it. Then he swore. He knew he hurt too much to be dead. Just like in 'Nam. The beacon was still working; he saw it blinking beside the far hatch. Mark listened, but couldn't hear the helicopter.

He gave one more try, pulling his torso across the tar of the roof. He lunged again and felt the edge of the hatchway scraping his hips, then his legs. At last he flopped out on top of the roof and was free. His legs felt better—but his damn chest! Whenever he lifted his arms it felt like six Viet Cong were playing field hockey with his ribcage.

Carefully he sat up, then tried to push the cover over the entrance. He couldn't. He crawled to the cold bottle and stared at it. The thermometer was broken, but it had read at exactly zero when it broke. That had to be cold enough to hold for ten more minutes. Where the hell was that chopper?

His watch showed he had two minutes to wait. Mark brought up the Uzi and set it for fully automatic fire, 600 rounds per minute. He took the last two fragmentation grenades from his pants and laid them on the roof. He could hear running feet below now. Mark waited another fifteen seconds. When the first shot came through the sky hatch, he pulled the pin on one of the M-3 fraggers and let the handle snap off, arming it and starting the timing fuse. In three seconds he dropped it through the hatch.

The grenade went off before it hit the floor. Two Black Gold noncoms died instantly on the ladder. Six more black soldiers crouched below for an all-out assault died slowly. All twelve men in the fourth-floor hall were wounded.

Mark tried to get to his feet. He couldn't. Instead he crawled, rolling the cold bottle ahead of him. It was fifty miles across the small roof to the beacon.

At last he made it, then remembered the last grenade was still near the hatch opening. Tough apples, as one of his old sergeants used to say. He swung the Uzi toward the open hatch and waited.

A minute later he heard the whup-whup-whup of the Hughes chopper coming in low over buildings. It had its navigation lights out now, Mark saw, but it homed in steadily on the beacon.

Shots came through the roof hatch. Mark took the .45 and stitched the opening with three rounds. The chopper came in, hovering a foot off the deck. Mark stood and heaved the bottle inside, behind the seats. The pilot had tied open the door. Mark grimaced as he bellied into the seat and rolled, letting the pilot help belt him in.

Mark turned and gave the hatch one last burst of automatic fire from the Uzi, then leaned back in the seat as they lifted straight up.

"Crazy, I haven't had this much fun since the damn DMZ in 'Nam," the pilot shouted.

As the chopper turned, Mark saw two figures leap from the hatch opening to the roof and shoulder rifles. The Penetrator sprayed the area with the last half-dozen rounds in the Uzi and saw the flash fifty yards below as one of the 9 mm parabellum slugs from the Uzi hit the M-3 grenade, detonating it. Only one shot had come at the chopper from the roof.

Then they were away, sliding over buildings as they moved out low to the Hudson river, then dropped mast-high and flew downstream.

Mark looked at the Uzi, shook his head and threw it out the open door.

"Hey, that was a valuable weapon," the pilot shouted.

"Right, but not worth spending thirty years in prison for," Mark said. He threw out the Hi-Standard and his Colt .45 Commander too. He would replace them all; it was better than taking a risk of getting picked up with them. He was clean.

"Buddy, I think we made it," Mark said. "Only one little problem left. That damn bottle."

"We're only four minutes from touchdown at the pad," the pilot said.

"Yeah, but that's a cryogenic bottle, a big fat cold bottle. The juice inside can't get to more than twenty degrees above zero or the whole thing blasts apart and the East Coast turns into one huge graveyard. You understand that?"

"Yeah, sure. But . . ."

"Get on your radio and patch through to the cops. Talk to Lt. Chuchulski. Tell him you have the bottle of goodies that Black Gold had, the one he's been hunting. Tell him to have a refrigerated truck at the 30th Street heliport as soon as he can get it there. Make it within five minutes. Tell him an ice cream truck, a milk wagon, anything insulated and refrigerated will do. Explain the goodies are in a cryogenic bottle that must be kept cold."

Mark felt a wave of greyness sweep over him. He held on, but a groan slipped out from tight lips.

"Hey, man, you hit? Pick up some lead?"

Mark wasn't sure what happened next. He didn't remember hearing anything, then he shook his head and saw that the lights had changed.

"Get the damn bottle to the cops soon as you can." Mark blinked. Dammit, he wasn't thinking clearly. Not following the damn game plan. He gave the pilot an arrowhead. Was it the first one? He couldn't remember.

"Hey, you remember what I look like? Cops are going to ask you."

The pilot grinned. "It was too damn dark. I didn't even see your face clearly."

"Remember that." Mark handed him the other thousand-dollar roll of bills and pointed to a park ahead on the New York side.

"Set down in that park for ten seconds, and let me fall out of here. Leave your lights off. Then get to that pad as flat out as you can go."

"Illegal as hell to land down there."

"Yeah, tough. Do it. Tell the cops last time you saw me I had just taken six slugs from a Chinese burp gun and was falling down that hatchway so you could get the bottle away. Tell them I'm damn well dead by now."

"Roger. That should take some heat off you," the pilot said. "Damn. I haven't had so much fun since I flew that jackass general around in 'Nam. He used to like to shadow our patrols on search and destroy missions. I got a rifle slug in my leg one day and he took one in the lung. Damn near killed him."

A minute later the chopper touched the soft grass and Mark stepped to the ground in the dark.

"Get that damn bottle to a refer fast. Tell the fuzz it's the X-447, but don't use that name on the air."

"Cops already got there with some kind of a portable box. You passed out for a couple of minutes when I talked to them."

Mark nodded and stood on the grass as the chopper lifted away. He thought he was in prtty good shape until the downdraft of the chopper hit him. It shoved him sideways and into the soft grass. He was glad there wasn't a foot of snow on the ground. Mark remembered to turn as he fell so he wouldn't hit his chest. Damn, it hurt. He flopped on the ground, knowing he should be moving if he had to crawl. Then he blacked out.

It was an hour before he came to. The cold night air roused him. The pain in his chest was five times as bad now. He had to get help. But first the disguise.

He reached behind his head and pulled off the tape that held the blond wig in place. Then he stripped the tight rubber "second skin" mask off his face. He snorted at the long scar on the mask's right cheek, the pockmarks on the forehead, and the built-up eyebrows and nose that had made him look entirely different.

He stuffed the mask and wig in one of the leg pockets, then wondered if he could walk.

Five minutes later he made it to his feet and began staggering toward a phone booth a hundred yards away. It took him almost a half hour to reach it. The last fifty yards he crawled. Then he called Joanna.

EPILOGUE

Mark Hardin winced as he lay back on the couch in Joanna's apartment. His call had come just as she had almost made up her mind to phone the cops with the 172nd Street address.

Joanna stood in the background, watching the cool, quick hands of Selma as she opened his flight suit and examined the wound. He had to be all right, he simply had to be, she told herself. She still didn't understand just why she cared so much for this man.

"Damn," Selma said. "You are one lucky sonofabitch, you know that, honkey?"

Mark blinked and looked at the person working over him. He really didn't care who she was. He knew someone else had helped Joanna get him into her car and up to her apartment. Now he blinked to clear his eyes and saw the girl was black. He shrugged, mentally.

"Joanna, look at this," Selma said. "The damn bullet went in clean, hit a rib and slanted under his tough white hide for almost eight inches before it finally came out his side. A quarter of an inch either way and this big hunk of man would be stretched out on some cold marble slab."

As she talked she worked with pads of cotton and alcohol, cleaning up the blood, putting dressings on the puncture wounds, and staring at old scars. She pressed on a spot near the bullet hole.

"This hurt, honey?"

Mark groaned.

"Does, huh? Okay, we got us one cracked rib to tape up. Outside of that I can clear you for humping with this broad in two days."

Joanna laughed, embarrassed. Suddenly she wished her good friend would shut up. Selma was a first class R.N. and a close friend of five years standing, but she was always horsing around, and she loved to talk dirty and embarrass Joanna.

But when you didn't want to go to a doctor with a bullet wound, Selma meant salvation. The black nurse had done several free-lance medical jobs for Joanna before. Now she watched Selma taping Mark's chest.

Ten minutes later the nurse had shot Mark with penicillin and tetanus toxoid and picked up her little black bag.

"Look, mama, you keep away from this stud for at least two days, y'all hear? He's got to keep up his strength."

Joanna caught her arm and pulled Selma to the door where she thanked her. Out of Mark's hearing, Selma changed, softened.

"Honey, don't worry about him, he'll be fine.

Change those dressings once a day and take the tape off in about a week." She grinned. "He is one beautiful hunk of man!"

Joanna thanked her again and closed the door. When she went back to see Mark he was sleeping.

An hour later he woke up and told her what had happened. She phoned Lt. Chuchulski. She finally tracked him down to a cold storage plant in Brooklyn. He told her the panic was over; they had the X-447 in safe hands. It was being freeze dried, and then the residue would be burned in an air-tight kiln until nothing but ashes remained. The ashes would be sealed in lead and buried fifteen miles down in the ground at the bottom of an old oil well. The well would be filled, sealed and capped.

He said they had sweated the chopper pilot until he told them the location of the Black Gold headquarters, but by the time they got there the place was half burned up. Firemen finished putting out the flames, and the police moved in to count the bodies and capture thirty men and over five hundred illegal arms, tons of ammunition, and blueprints for a massive takeover of the state.

"Did you find the Penetrator?"

"The pilot told us he left him dying on the roof. We're not sure, but one of the bodies could be his. A dozen or so were burned beyond any hope of telling even what color their skin was. So we're listing him as one of the dead. We got a good description of him we'll put on the wire: blonde, six-two, scar on his cheek, bulging eyebrows and a hook nose. If he shows up anywhere we'll spot him."

Joanna thanked the officer and hung up.

Mark heard just enough of it to understand. He

knew the pilot would talk. Once he felt the spotlight and the publicity he'd tell them everything he could remember. He'd even invite the cops to lift prints off the chopper. But they wouldn't help because he'd had on his semi-permeable gloves. He looked up at the woman.

"You're staying here, of course, until I can nurse you back to health," she said. She sat beside him on the couch.

"Who was your black medic?"

"Friend who helps me from time to time."

"She's wild."

She bent and kissed him, and his arms came up slowly. It was a long kiss.

When he let her go, she stood, staring down at him. She really hadn't meant to let it come to this. Her whole body had reacted instantly to his embrace.

She took a deep breath and swallowed. "Oh, I have a message from a friend of yours. He says to be careful."

"What friend?"

"Dan Griggs." Her smile developed into a giggle.

Mark scowled. "When did you know?"

"Not until yesterday. I was checking with Dan by phone about something else, and he asked me if I'd seen anybody that looked like you. He knew you were in town by the papers. He described you, told me how you operate."

"Then you *are* with Justice?"

"I work for Diogenes Investigations."

"A front. You have too many computers, too many good connections. No other private operation an get F.B.I. criminal printouts."

Joanna smiled and looked at the small bottle of

pain pills Selma had left. She took out two and brought a glass of water. "Mark Hardin, that's your name, right?" She went on. "Mark, if I were with Justice you know I couldn't tell you, right? So let's just say that I didn't tell you I'm with Justice."

Mark took both pills without question. That could get a guy killed. But she had that kind of an effect on him.

"Think Dan will let you off for a few days?"

"I've already called in sick with the five-day flu."

He smiled. More and more, this girl was infiltrating those very private places which he had been so sure no one could ever touch again. He felt his body reacting to the drugs and the continuing pain. It would take him a couple of days to get on his feet and feel like flying again. Maybe they could take a little trip together.

"Miami is nice this time of year. Maybe we could fly down there for a couple of days."

She sat down and took his hand. "Maybe we can. But that's a long way off. Why don't we just take it a day at a time, and see what happens."

He nodded and felt sleep coming. Again she had said exactly the right thing. He watched this beautiful girl until his eyes closed. He didn't feel much like the Penetrator right then. Crime would have to get along without him for a few days. He had a big hurt, and he had just found out that he could feel strongly for a woman again.

Tomorrow they would talk. Tomorrow. Mark let it all slip away as he thought of Joanna. He smiled as he slept.

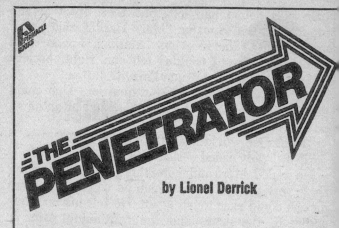

THE PENETRATOR

by Lionel Derrick

Mark Hardin. Discharged from the army, after service in Vietnam. His military career was over. But *his* war was just beginning. His reason for living and reason for dying become the same—to stamp out crime and corruption wherever he finds it. He is deadly; he is unpredictable; and he is dedicated. He is The Penetrator!

Read all of him in:

_____	P00236-X	THE TARGET IS H, No. 1	.95
_____	P00237-8	BLOOD ON THE STRIP, No. 2	.95
_____	P00318-8	CAPITOL HELL, No. 3	.95

TO ORDER

Please check the space next to the book/s you want, send this order form together with your check or money order, include the price of the book/s and 15¢ for handling and mailing to:

PINNACLE BOOKS INC. / P.O. Box 4347
Grand Central Station / New York, N.Y. 10017

☐ CHECK HERE IF YOU WANT A FREE CATALOG.

I have enclosed $_____ check_____ or money order_____ as payment in full. No C.O.D.'s.

Name_____

Address_____

City_____ State_____ Zip_____
(Please allow time for delivery)

the Executioner

PINNACLE BOOKS

The gutsiest, most exciting hero in years. Imagine a guy at war with the Godfather and all his Mafioso relatives! He's rough, he's deadly, he's a law unto himself — nothing and nobody stops him!

THE EXECUTIONER SERIES by DON PENDLETON

ORDER		TITLE	BOOK NO.	PRICE
_____	# 1	WAR AGAINST THE MAFIA	P401	$1.25
_____	# 2	DEATH SQUAD	P402	$1.25
_____	# 3	BATTLE MASK	P403	$1.25
_____	# 4	MIAMI MASSACRE	P404	$1.25
_____	# 5	CONTINENTAL CONTRACT	P405	$1.25
_____	# 6	ASSAULT ON SOHO	P406	$1.25
_____	# 7	NIGHTMARE IN NEW YORK	P407	$1.25
_____	# 8	CHICAGO WIPEOUT	P408	$1.25
_____	# 9	VEGAS VENDETTA	P409	$1.25
_____	#10	CARIBBEAN KILL	P410	$1.25
_____	#11	CALIFORNIA HIT	P411	$1.25
_____	#12	BOSTON BLITZ	P412	$1.25
_____	#13	WASHINGTON I.O.U.	P413	$1.25
_____	#14	SAN DIEGO SIEGE	P414	$1.25
_____	#15	PANIC IN PHILLY	P415	$1.25
_____	#16	SICILIAN SLAUGHTER	P416	$1.25
_____	#17	JERSEY GUNS	P328	$1.25
_____	#18	TEXAS STORM	P353	$1.25

AND MORE TO COME . . .

TO ORDER

Please check the space next to the book/s you want, send this order form together with your check or money order, include the price of the book/s and 15¢ for handling and mailing, to:

PINNACLE BOOKS, INC. / P.O. Box 4347
Grand Central Station / New York, N.Y. 10017

☐ CHECK HERE IF YOU WANT A FREE CATALOG.

I have enclosed $_____ check _____ or money order _____ as payment in full. No C.O.D.'s.

Name _____

Address _____

City _____ State _____ Zip _____

(Please allow time for delivery.)

ALL NEW DYNAMITE SERIES

THE DESTROYER

by Richard Sapir & Warren Murphy

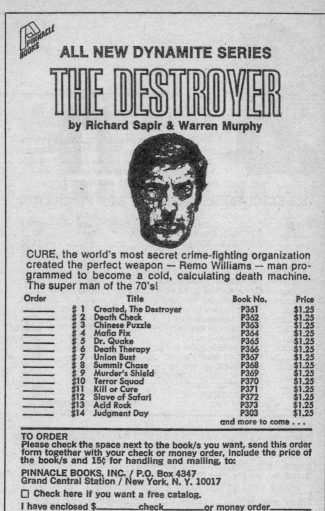

CURE, the world's most secret crime-fighting organization created the perfect weapon — Remo Williams — man programmed to become a cold, calculating death machine. The super man of the 70's!

Order		Title	Book No.	Price
_____	# 1	Created, The Destroyer	P361	$1.25
_____	# 2	Death Check	P362	$1.25
_____	# 3	Chinese Puzzle	P363	$1.25
_____	# 4	Mafia Fix	P364	$1.25
_____	# 5	Dr. Quake	P365	$1.25
_____	# 6	Death Therapy	P366	$1.25
_____	# 7	Union Bust	P367	$1.25
_____	# 8	Summit Chase	P368	$1.25
_____	# 9	Murder's Shield	P369	$1.25
_____	#10	Terror Squad	P370	$1.25
_____	#11	Kill or Cure	P371	$1.25
_____	#12	Slave of Safari	P372	$1.25
_____	#13	Acid Rock	P373	$1.25
_____	#14	Judgment Day	P303	$1.25

and more to come . . .

TO ORDER
Please check the space next to the book/s you want, send this order form together with your check or money order, include the price of the book/s and 15¢ for handling and mailing, to:

PINNACLE BOOKS, INC. / P.O. Box 4347
Grand Central Station / New York, N. Y. 10017

☐ **Check here if you want a free catalog.**

I have enclosed $_____ check _____ or money order _____ as payment in full. No C.O.D.s.

Name _____

Address _____

City _____ State _____ Zip _____

(Please allow time for delivery.)

PINNACLE
BOOKS

THE INCREDIBLE ACTION-PACKED SERIES

by Joseph Rosenberger

His name is Richard Camellion; he's a master of disguise, deception and destruction. He does what the CIA and FBI cannot do. They call him THE DEATH MERCHANT!

Order		Title	Book No.	Price
_____	#1	The Death Merchant	P021N	95¢
_____	#2	Operation Overkill	P085N	95¢
_____	#3	The Psychotron Plot	P117N	95¢
_____	#4	Chinese Conspiracy	P168N	95¢
_____	#5	Satan Strike	P182N	95¢
_____	#6	The Albanian Connection	P218N	95¢
_____	#7	The Castro File	P264N	95¢
			and more to come . . .	

TO ORDER

Please check the space next to the book/s you want, send this order form together with your check or money order, include the price of the book/s and 15¢ for handling and mailing, to:

PINNACLE BOOKS, INC. / P.O. Box 4347
Grand Central Station / New York, N. Y. 10017

☐ Check here if you want a free catalog.

I have enclosed $_____check_____or money order_____ as payment in full. No C.O.D.'s.

Name_____

Address_____

City_____State_____Zip_____
(Please allow time for delivery.)

PINNACLE
BOOKS

THE "BUTCHER,"
the only man to leave
the Mafia—and live!
A man forever on the run,
unable to trust anyone,
condemned to a life
of constant violence!

THE BUTCHER SERIES

by Stuart Jason

Order		Title	Book No.	Price
_____	#1	KILL QUICK OR DIE	P011	95¢
_____	#2	COME WATCH HIM DIE	P025	95¢
_____	#3	KEEPERS OF DEATH	P084	95¢
_____	#4	BLOOD DEBT	P111	95¢
_____	#5	DEADLY DEAL	P152	95¢
_____	#6	KILL TIME	P197	95¢
_____	#7	DEATH RACE	P228	95¢
_____	#8	FIRE BOMB	P272	95¢
_____	#9	SEALED WITH BLOOD	P279	95¢
_____	#10	THE DEADLY DOCTOR	P291	95¢

and more to come . . .

TO ORDER

Please check the space next to the book/s you want, send this order
form together with your check or money order, include the price of
the book/s and 15¢ for handling and mailing, to:

PINNACLE BOOKS, INC. / P.O. Box 4347
Grand Central Station / New York, N. Y. 10017

☐ Check here if you want a free catalog.

I have enclosed $_____check_____or money order_____
as payment in full. No C.O.D.'s.

Name_____

Address_____

City_____State_____Zip_____
(Please allow time for delivery.)

PINNACLE BOOKS

EXCITING NEW ADVENTURE SERIES!
crackling tension, slick and explosive

the private army of colonel robin

The deadliest
fighting force
in the world!
For hire,
they'll fight wars
anywhere!

By Alan Caillou

Order		Title	Book No.	Price
_____	#1	Dead Sea Submarine	P015	95¢
_____	#2	Terror in Rio	P035	95¢
_____	#3	Congo War Cry	.P071	95¢
_____	#4	Afghan Assault	P097	95¢
_____	#5	Swamp War	P164	95¢
_____	#6	Death Charge	P268	95¢
			and more to come . . .	

TO ORDER
Please check the space next to the book/s you want, send this order
form together with your check or money order, include the price of
the book/s and 15¢ for handling and mailing, to:

PINNACLE BOOKS, INC. / P.O. Box 4347
Grand Central Station / New York, N. Y. 10017

☐ Check here if you want a free catalog.

I have enclosed $_____check_____or money order_____
as payment in full. No. C.O.D.s.

Name_____

Address_____

City_____State_____Zip_____

(Please allow time for delivery.)

THE RAZONI & JACKSON SERIES

One's black, one's white—they're young and the ballsiest detectives on the city beat! Dynamite—and exclusively from Pinnacle!

by W. B. MURPHY

Order	Book No.	Title	Price
____	P00163-O	CITY IN HEAT, #1	95¢
____	P00194-O	DEAD END STREET, #2	95¢
____	P00267-X	ONE NIGHT STAND, #3	95¢

and more to come . . .

TO ORDER
Please check the space next to the book/s you want, send this order form together with your check or money order, include the price of the book/s and 15¢ for handling and mailing to:

PINNACLE BOOKS, INC. / P.O. Box 4347
Grand Central Station / New York, N.Y. 10017
☐ CHECK HERE IF YOU WANT A FREE CATALOG.

I have enclosed $_____check_____or money order_____
as payment in full. No C.O.D.'s.

Name____,_____

Address_____

City_____State_____Zip____
(Please allow time for delivery.)